JF
MARTIN

mystery

Martin, Ann M.,
1955–

Missing since
Monday

$12.95

3/98

6/97

MISSING SINCE
MONDAY

Other Books by Ann M. Martin

With You and Without You
Me and Katie (the Pest)
Stage Fright
Inside Out
Bummer Summer

Ann M. Martin

MISSING SINCE MONDAY

Holiday House / New York

The author gratefully acknowledges Carolyn
Zogg, Associate Director of Child Find, Inc.,
and Eric M. Perkins, Esq., for their sensitive
evaluations of the manuscript.

Library of Congress Cataloging-in-Publication
Data

Martin, Ann M.
Missing since Monday.

SUMMARY: When their little sister doesn't come
home from school, fifteen-year-old Maggie and
her brother must face up to some deep, dark
secrets about their natural mother, whom they
must consider as a kidnapping suspect.
    [1. Kidnapping—Fiction]   I. Title.
PZ7.M3567585Mi   1986   [Fic]   86-45390
ISBN 0-8234-0626-1

This book is for the second generation
of Kentucky cousins:
LYMAN MARTIN CREASON
WILLIAM SCOTT CREASON
JOSHUA CALVIN MARCUS
COURTENAY ROBERTSON MARTIN
and
ELEANOR HANCOCK MARTIN

Contents

MISSING SINCE MONDAY

1

Leigh

"Hi, Leigh! We're home!" I called.

"Hi, honey," my stepmother answered. "I'm in my studio."

"Okay," I called back. I turned to Courtenay. "Want to go see Mommy?" I asked, closing the front door behind us.

Courtenay nodded and licked the last sticky remains of a piece of peppermint candy from her fingers. As far as she was concerned, the candy had been the high point of our late-afternoon outing. I'd taken her on a walk all the way to the elementary school playground to ride on the swings and the merry-go-round and the seesaw. Walking back, I'd given her the candy. Just one piece. It had made her day.

"Come on, Miss Messy Face," I said, smiling.

"I am not a messy-face."

"Yes, you are. Stick out your tongue."

Courtie obliged.

"It's as red as a radish," I informed her.

She giggled. "I want to show Mommy!" she cried, and ran up the stairs to the second floor of our house and into the studio where Leigh does her illustrating.

Leigh turned around as Courtie skipped in. "Hello, sweetheart! Did you have a g— What on *earth?*" she exclaimed.

"What?" I said. I had followed Courtenay into the studio and couldn't see anything out of the ordinary. I glanced around in search of whatever it was Leigh saw, but she was looking at Courtenay.

"What do you mean, 'what'!" repeated Leigh. "Look at your sister." (Courtenay is really my half sister, but we don't make a big thing of it.)

I glanced at her. She looked fine—just dirty enough to indicate she'd had a lot of fun that afternoon, which she had.

"She's filthy! Where did you take her?"

"I took her to the dump, Leigh," I said. "She had a fabulous time. She played in mountains of trash and rode around in a garbage truck, okay?"

"There's no need for sarcasm, Maggie. Just give me a straight answer. Is that possible?"

"I give up. Is it?" I said.

Leigh looked ready to strangle me. Courtie was glancing warily back and forth between her mother and me, trying to figure out what was going on. All she was sure of was that we were bickering again.

But for heaven's sake. Okay, so Courtie had some dirt on the knees of her pants, and a piece of grass in her hair and a little red around her mouth. She was four. What did Leigh expect? Four-year-olds get dirty. I'd be more worried if she were pristine every day. To me, dirt is a sign of fun. It's normal.

"And what's she been eating?" Leigh went on. "What did you have to eat, baby?" she asked Courtenay, in case I still wouldn't give her a straight answer.

"Candy," said Courtenay cautiously, glancing up at me.

"Candy!" cried Leigh. "Oh, *Maggie*. She's going to ruin her teeth before she gets to kindergarten."

"They're her baby teeth. She'll lose them even if they're cavity-free."

Leigh was determined to find fault with what I'd done. "Well, it's five o'clock. What about her dinner? Her appetite's probably ruined."

"I doubt it," I said. "She only ate one piece."

Leigh sighed heavily. She pulled Courtenay to her and gave her a hug. "Oh, baby." She rocked her back and forth.

Gag, gag.

I really love Courtie. And I love Leigh, too, I guess. After all, she'd been my stepmother for five years then, ever since I was eleven, and she'd seen my older brother, Mike, and me through some hard times. But Leigh and I had always clashed, especially over Courtenay. See, Leigh didn't quite trust me. We got off on the wrong foot and never seemed to get on the right one, at least not for long.

We had very different opinions about young children. I believe in letting them play and have fun and eat junk food every now and then and go to bed late if there's nothing important to get up for the next morning. But Leigh had overprotected Courtenay. She watched her like a hawk and practically fainted if so much as a granule of sugar went in her mouth or if she got in bed past eight o'clock. She was going to give the kid a complex.

I may get one myself. I mean, Leigh really did overreact to things. Here's how we got off on the wrong foot: I was ten years old the day we met, and after Leigh had given Mike and me each a present, she said brightly, "Well, why don't we take a walk and get to know each other?"

And I said, "No, thank you," because I'd promised my new friend Jane we would make doll clothes later that afternoon. A walk sounded like it might take up just enough time so that it would cut into the clothes-making, and I have this thing about breaking promises. But before I had a chance to explain that, Leigh began to look all hurt and resentful and suspicious. Six years later, even though we got along pretty well most of the time, that hurt and resentment and suspicion were always there, running under the surface of our relationship like a polluted current.

Furthermore, because Courtenay is Leigh's only natural child, Leigh used to be super-super-protec-

tive of her. I had *never* done a thing that had put
Courtenay in any kind of danger, and she'd never had
an accident worse than a skinned knee while I was
taking care of her, but Leigh didn't trust me because
of the candy and the grass stains and stuff. But really.
What was Courtenay—a china doll or a child?

In a few days, Dad and Leigh were going away on
their long-overdue honeymoon. They were leaving
Mike and me in charge of Courtenay, but Leigh had
fought long and hard to get someone older to stay
with us for that week. She just didn't trust us. Luckily
her mother, the unusual Mrs. Simon, was in Europe,
because Mike and I would have died at the idea of
having her stay with us. I mean, Mike would be in
college in the fall, and I was a sophomore in high
school.

So, against Leigh's better judgment, we won the
right to take full care of Courtenay for a week. I was
looking forward to it. I like dressing Courtenay and
playing with her and taking her shopping. She's a
neat little kid.

"Maggie?" Leigh's voice snapped me from my
thoughts.

"Yeah?" I replied dully.

"I'm sorry, honey. Let's not argue. I'll clean Courtie
up and start dinner. Why don't you do your homework?"

"Okay." I grinned at Courtie, who beamed back,
and I gave Leigh a peck on the cheek, glad that all
seemed forgiven. Then I went to my room, but not to

do my homework. I could do it after dinner. I just wanted time to be alone with my thoughts.

I closed the door softly and lay down on my bed, resting against the throw pillows Leigh had helped me to make, and thought about my family, about Leigh and my real mother.

Mike and I have lived with Dad ever since my mom took off when I was seven. They got divorced a year later. I love my mom and I know she loves Mike and me. Of course, I haven't seen her in ages, but that's just because she's such a creative person, and creative people need space. At least, some of them do. Well, Mom seems to. She's too...too...I don't know what. Actually, I don't really remember her, which is interesting, considering she did live with us until I was seven. Anyway, she's just one of those people who has so much energy she has to be moving and going all the time. So she travels around the country and drops Mike and me a postcard every now and then. I wish I had her energy.

The last postcard she'd sent reached me a month ago. It was postmarked California and it said: "Dear Maggie, How are you? I'm fine. I have a job as a waitress now in Beeman's Café." That surprised me, because I'd thought my mother was in Michigan taking pottery classes. I'd been writing her there for the past three months. "Be good and do what Owen tells you. Love, Mom." (Owen is Dad.)

One ironic thing is that Mike and I are the spitting image of our mother (or so we've been told). I can't tell much from the few fuzzy black-and-white photos we have here and there. At any rate, we look nothing like Courtenay and not much like Dad. Courtenay has a pixie face, brown eyes, and tawny hair. Mike and I look as Irish as shamrocks, with red hair, blue eyes, and fair complexions. And I've got enough freckles on my body to share with half the world. We look like misfits when the rest of the family is around.

Anyway, Dad married Leigh five years ago after Leigh's disastrous first marriage ended with a divorce, and one year later, Courtenay was born. The reason Dad and Leigh were going on their honeymoon five years late was that they hadn't had a decent one after they'd been married—just a weekend at an inn in Vermont. They they'd rushed back to Mike and me and their jobs, and a year later, they'd had Courtenay.

I love Dad's and Leigh's jobs, especially Leigh's. Leigh illustrates children's books. She's pretty well known. She works right out of our house in Princeton, New Jersey. And she works hard. She even put Courtenay in a special school program so that she would have enough time each day to do her work.

We have a big house, and the room on the second floor that used to be the sewing room is now Leigh's studio. It has good light and enough space for her drawing boards and easels, her paints and inks, brushes and pens, boards and rulers.

My dad is in publishing. He commutes to New York City on the train every day. He's a big-time editor at a

very successful company that publishes hardcover
children's books and adult books. Dad is the publisher of the children's books. He knows Judy Blume
and Maurice Sendak. Once he met Roald Dahl.

I guess it's because of Dad that Mike and I are such
big readers. We always have been. Dad used to bring
home bags full of children's books from his office
when we were little. We couldn't get enough of them.
Now he just brings them home for Courtenay, since
Mike and I read adult books.

My brother is very smart and *very* funny. I've
always been drawn to a sense of humor in people.
And he's a good big brother. He let me follow him
around when we were little. Now that we're older,
we're just good pals. And we made a lot of the same
friends after we moved from our old house on Herrontown Road when Mom and Dad split up. For in-
stance, my boyfriend is David Jacobssen. He's a year
older than I am. His twin sister, Martha, is my best
friend. And Mike's best friend, Andrew de Christopher, is the older brother of Jane de Christopher,
who is a good friend of Martha's and mine. We all
kind of hang around together.

Knock, knock, knock.

"Come in," I called.

The door opened and Courtie bounced into my
room and flung herself on my bed. "Dinner's ready,
dinner's ready!" she announced.

"Already? Is Dad home?"

"Yup."

I'd been daydreaming longer than I thought.

Courtie climbed on my back, and I gave her a piggyback ride into the dining room.

"Mommymommymommymommy!"

Late that night, Courtenay's wails shattered the silence, and I jerked awake. I hoped Leigh would get up soon. If she didn't, I would.

"Mommy!...Mommy?"

I rolled out of bed and stumbled across my room to the door, not bothering to turn on a light. Courtenay was crying hard. She must have been either sick or hurt.

I thrust open the door to her room and switched on the Three Little Kittens lamp on her dresser.

"Courtie?" I asked softly.

She lay on her bed in a wild mess of sheets and blankets. Her hair was drenched with sweat.

I put my hand on her forehead. "Courtenay, what's wrong? Are you sick?" She felt warm but not feverish.

"It's back," she sobbed. "It's under my bed right now. Pull your feet up, Maggie. Pull your feet up."

I obeyed. "What's under the bed?"

"The red mitten."

Oh, no. Not that old nightmare. "The red mitten that snores?" I asked.

"Yes, yes!"

I gathered Courtenay in my arms and held her. "That's just a dream, a bad dream," I reminded her. Courtie hadn't dreamed about the red mitten that snores in months. We thought she'd finally outgrown it. "Remember what we said about bad dreams?"

"They're not real," replied Courtenay automatically, brushing her tears from her damp face. "But the red mitten that snores is down there. It's under my bed."

"No, it's not. I'll show you," I replied.

I was on my hands and knees with my head under Courtenay's bed when Leigh finally came in.

"Mommy!" cried Courtie. "It's back." Fresh tears started to fall.

I withdrew my head and looked up at Leigh. "The red mitten that snores," I said flatly.

"Oh, baby," murmured Leigh. She sat cross-legged in the middle of the bed and took Courtenay into her lap. She rocked her back and forth, back and forth. After a few moments, Leigh signaled me that Courtie was already falling asleep, so I tiptoed out of the room and back into my own bed.

I looked at my watch. Two-thirty. I really should go back to sleep soon or I'd be a basket case at school tomorrow, I thought, but I was avoiding nightmares of my own. I had them pretty often, more often than Courtenay did. I knew they weren't real, I knew they wouldn't hurt me, but they still scared me to death. Sometimes, if I fought sleep until my eyes were heavy and my head was fuzzy, I would fall into such an exhausted sleep that I would be too tired for nightmares. That was just what I did on the red-mitten night.

2

On Our Own

Two mornings later, Dad and Leigh left on their long-awaited honeymoon. They were spending it on the island of Saint Barthélemy in the Caribbean. To get there, they had to drive to Newark Airport, park their car, take a plane to Miami, Florida, and then to the island of Saint Martin, and finally take a boat to Saint Bart's (as it's called). It was going to be a long trip, and Leigh said she'd probably be airsick or seasick or both.

Dad and Leigh left at six o'clock in the morning, so Mike and I were in charge of Courtenay from the time she woke up.

"I'll dress her this morning," I said to Mike, "and you start breakfast. We can switch chores every day."

I looked in Courtenay's closet and chose one of her new outfits—baggy lavender pants with cuffs at the ankles, and a pink-and-lavender striped sweatshirt.

"What shall we do with your hair today?" I asked
Courtenay.

Courtenay has very pretty hair—thick and tawny,
and just long enough for braids or ponytails.

"One big braid!" said Courtenay.

"Okay. Coming up."

Courtenay giggled. Then stopped. She tried to turn
around and tried to look at me as I stood behind her,
working on her hair.

"Face forward, Courtie," I told her. "Otherwise
your braid will be crooked."

"But where're Mommy and Daddy?" she wanted
to know.

"They've gone on a trip. Remember?"

"Yeah," said Courtenay uncertainly.

"And Mike and I are going to take care of you,
right?"

"Right!"

By the time Courtenay and I came downstairs,
Mike had breakfast ready. And what a breakfast!
When he gets a chance to cook, he really goes to it. I
hate to cook. My idea of cooking is opening a can of
soup and defrosting frozen vegetables. Toast is about
all I can manage for breakfast. But Mike had made
pancakes and bacon, fresh orange juice, coffee for
himself and me, and hot chocolate for Courtenay.

"Oh, yum-yum-yum!" she exclaimed. I felt the
same way.

As we ate our breakfast, I began playing the Lost
Game with Courtenay. "Okay, Courtie. Let's pre-
tend."

"Goody," she said. "I'm lost, right?"

"Right. What's the first thing you do?"

"Look for a policeman."

"Yay! One point! And if you can't find a policeman, do you tell just any adult?"

"No!"

"Yay! Another point. What do you look for instead?"

"A telephone!"

"Yay! Another point. How many is that?" I asked Mike.

"Three," he replied. "Okay, now for the big one. What's your phone number?"

Courtenay took a deep breath and began singing the song we'd taught her. "Five-one-nine-five-five-five-two-eight-three-six. That's my phone number, that's my phone number!" We had taught her how to use both a dial phone and a push-button phone.

"All *right!* That gets you five points, for a total of eight. Now, Jay," said Mike to an imaginary announcer, "tell our contestant what we have behind the curtain... That's right, it's a new washer-dryer with a special blender attachment. A surprise package chosen especially for you, worth... over one *thousand* dollars!"

The game went on. Mike and I ran through everything we thought Courtenay should know about being on her own in the big, bad world: who to trust, who not to trust, what to do if somebody wanted to give her candy, touch her, take her for a ride....

And that was one of the big problems between Leigh and me. Leigh was incensed that I had started the Lost Game. She thought it would scare Courtenay, and all Leigh wanted to do was protect her.

"But *I'm* protecting her, too," I argued one day. "Did you see that TV show last night? The one about child abuse and missing kids? Every day little kids are stolen or molested or—"

"Maggie! Enough!" Leigh had exclaimed. "That kind of thing does not happen around here. Not in little Princeton. All we have to do is keep an eye on Courtenay, not scare her to death with foolish thoughts about strangers or getting lost. Now stop."

I didn't stop, though. I just didn't do it in front of Leigh anymore. But Leigh knew it went on anyway, and it made her pretty angry.

At that moment the phone rang. I answered it and my heart leaped. It was David!

"Listen," he said, "are you free tomorrow night? You want to go to a movie?"

"I'd love to. Let me see what Mike's doing." I covered the mouthpiece of the phone. "Mike?" I asked. "What are you doing tomorrow night?"

"Oh, Courtenay and I are going to sit around, play some poker, have a couple of beers, maybe smoke a good cigar—"

I burst out laughing. "No, really."

"I'm going to the movies."

"Oh," I said, feeling disappointed. "David just asked *me* to go to the movies."

"Well, why don't we have everyone over here instead? Courtie told me she's always wanted to go to a toga party."

"Mike!" I was laughing again. Then I became serious. "Wait a second. No. If Leigh finds out we had a party while we were supposed to be in charge of Courtenay, she'll—" I broke off, noticing that Courtenay was listening to our conversation with great interest. "Well, you know."

"I was *kidding*," Mike said. "We'll just have a few friends over. For pizza or something. Not a big blowout."

"Well . . . if we ask Andrew and Jane, do we have to ask Brad?" Brad is Andrew and Jane's older brother who always wants to hang around with us.

Mike made a face. Nobody likes Brad because he's always either getting people in trouble by ratting on them or making people shut up by blackmailing them. Personally, I think he's slime. "Of course not," said Mike. "No one wants him around."

I uncovered the mouthpiece. "Mike was going to go out tomorrow night," I told David, "but then he suggested that we have everyone over here for a party instead. We could get a pizza or something."

"Oh, okay," said David. "Sounds great. I'll tell Martha."

So the weekend got off to a good start.

I hung up the phone and handed Courtenay her lunch. Then Mike and I stood on the front steps and watched her climb into the little van that she rode to school each day. I shaded my eyes to take a look at the driver, but he wasn't one I knew. There are about six people, all retired, who volunteer to drive the buses to Courtenay's school, so I never knew who

was going to pick her up and drop her off. Leigh
knew all the drivers, though. "You see?" she'd said
once. "This is how you keep Courtenay safe. You just
have to know things, like who the drivers are."

But that seemed too simple to me.

Anyway, Mike and I went off to school ourselves,
and that afternoon we returned as soon as our last
class was over. Then I waited for Courtenay's bus
while Mike drove downtown to the grocery store. We
needed milk, cereal, apples, and stuff for the get-
together.

While I sat on the front steps watching for Courtenay's bus, I went through the mail. There were bills
for Dad and Leigh, two letters for Leigh from publishing companies she worked for, magazines, ads—
and a postcard to me from Mom! I read it quickly. Her
postcards never said much. This one said: "Dearest
Maggie, How are you? How is Mike? I'm still in California, waitressing. I hope school is going okay. Be a
good girl. Love, Mom."

Beep, beep!

I looked up when I heard the horn and the sound of
something pulling into our driveway. It was Courtenay's bus, and her favorite driver was at the wheel.

I ran to meet them. "Hi, Birdie!" I called to the
driver. Birdie is this wonderful skinny old woman
with a heap of dyed red hair piled on her head, and
false lashes so long they must weigh her eyelids
down. She's seventy-five years old and acts sixteen.
She's never been married, but she loves kids, so driv-

ing the bus is fun for her. A lark, as she puts it.

"Hiya, honey!" she called back. "I got your little sister here, safe and sound."

Courtenay bounded down the steps of the bus, clutching her lunchbox and various art projects.

"'Bye, Birdie!" she cried.

"Goodbye, honey. Have a swell weekend."

Birdie always says things like "swell" and "lark" and "terrif" and "natch." "Natch" means "naturally."

"Okay," said Courtenay, grinning.

"You have a good one, too," I told Birdie.

"Thanks, honey."

And we did have a swell weekend. Well, mostly swell.

3

The Weekend

On Friday we had a nightmare night like the one we'd had on Wednesday. It started at two o'clock with Courtenay screaming about the red mitten that snores. Then, just like the other night, after she'd been calmed down and was asleep again, I went back to my room. I tried to stay awake but fell right into a hideous dream.

When it was over, I lay shivering and sweating and wanting only for the night to be over so daylight would put an end to the dream demons.

Before I knew it, the night *was* over. I was curled up in my bed, the sheets and blanket twisted hotly around me. Sun was filtering through the curtains, pushing its way around the shades. And a voice at the foot of my bed said, "I'm hungry."

I jumped. The dream demons were still with me.

"Is it breakfast yet?" asked the voice.

Only Courtenay.

"Come here, monkey," I said, and Courtenay, half dressed, hurled herself at me, giggling and wiggling.

"How was your night?" I asked her. "Is the red mitten gone?"

"No, it's still under my bed. It lives there, you know. I had to jump out of bed this morning like this, so it wouldn't get my feet." Courtenay demonstrated by leaping ungracefully off my bed, landing as far out in the room as she could manage.

"Courtie," I said thoughtfully, "if the red mitten snores all the time, then you know what? That means it's asleep. And if it's asleep, it can't hurt you."

"Yes, it can. It doesn't matter if it snores. It snores while it's awake. It's a magic mitten. A *mean* magic mitten."

"A mighty mean magic mitten," I added.

Courtenay began to giggle. I noticed that she forgot to stay away from her bed when we went into her room to finish getting her dressed. The red mitten was temporarily gone, banished to join Courtenay's dream demons in whatever place dream demons disappear to during daylight.

A little while later, Mike, Courtie, and I had just settled down to bowls of Grape Nuts in the kitchen when the phone rang. "I'll get it! Let me get it!" cried Courtenay urgently.

"You have a boyfriend or something?" asked Mike as the phone rang again.

But Courtenay didn't hear him. In her mad struggle

to stand in her chair, she knocked her entire bowl of cereal to the floor. Milk and Grape Nuts ran into her lap, splattering everywhere, and the bowl broke into six pieces.

R-i-i-ing.

"Courtenay Lou*ise!*" I said sharply.

Courtenay burst into tears. The phone rang a fourth time.

I snatched it off the hook. *"Hello,"* I barked.

I heard a hollow, airy sound and some static.

"Hello?" said a distant voice. "Is that you, Maggie?"

I forced myself to calm down and sound normal. "Leigh! Hi. How are you and Dad? Are you having fun? Is the weather nice?"

"Beautiful, honey. We're having a great time. We're both going to be burned to a crisp. How are you guys doing? How's Courtenay?"

I glanced at Courtie. Mike had actually put her into the kitchen sink and was hosing her down using the spray nozzle. She was wet, messy, and tear-stained.

"Oh, she's fine," I said. "We're just having breakfast."

"Can I talk to her, please?"

I hesitated. "She's kind of messy, Leigh."

"Maggie, just for a moment. We've never been separated this long before."

"All right." I put my hand over the mouthpiece and whispered, "Mike, Leigh wants to talk to Courtenay."

Mike didn't know what else to do. He stripped

Courtie, tried to dry her off with a dish towel, and set her, naked, in my chair. I handed her the phone. "It's Mommy," I told her.

"Hi, Mommy!" cried Courtenay, her tears forgotten.

Leigh must have asked her what she was doing because Courtenay said, "I'm having breakfast. I'm naked."

My heart sank. There was a pause. Then Courtie said, "Because I spilled my cereal." Another pause. Then, "Answering the phone."

If my heart sank any further, it would exit from my body through my toes.

Courtenay handed the phone back to me. "Mommy wants to talk to you again."

I'd had a feeling she would. "Leigh?"

"Maggie! What on earth is going on? Courtenay is sitting at the table *naked?* I certainly hope no one comes to the door. And she is *not* supposed to answer the phone, young lady. You know that. You never know who could be on the other end."

"Leigh, all she was going to do was find out who the call was for. It's no big deal."

"And what if it had been an obscene caller? You want her to listen to dirty talk? She may *not* answer the phone. Do you understand me?" Leigh's voice was shaking. "She's my child, not yours, and *I* make the rules. Try to show a little responsibility."

"Okay, okay. Here, Mike wants to say hello."

He didn't, but I had to get off the phone. I handed it to him, and he made a face at me. I went to my

room. It took me a half an hour to collect myself
enough to return to the kitchen. When I did, I found
the mess cleaned up, Courtenay dressed, and fresh
coffee waiting for me.

"Let's start the morning over again," I suggested.

Mike and Courtenay nodded. And as Mike handed
me the coffee, he held an imaginary microphone
to his mouth. "Jay, what consolation prize do we
have for the lady?... That's right, it's rich, aromatic,
mountain-grown coffee, a year's supply, valued at
one hundred dollars. Better luck next time."

By seven o'clock that evening, Mike and I were
ready for our friends to come over. We'd ordered two
large pizzas, one plain, one with everything except
anchovies, and we'd promised Courtenay she could
have a piece as soon as they arrived. David and
Martha were going to pick the pizzas up on their way
over to our house.

We'd bought soda and potato chips and M&Ms, and
Mike had made a big salad to go with the pizzas.
We'd gotten out our Trivial Pursuit game and selected
two funny movies to play on the VCR later. For the
time being, our television was turned to MTV. We
were all set.

The phone rang and I jumped.

"Can you get that?" Mike called from the
bathroom. Courtenay was absorbed in a video and
hadn't even heard the phone ring.

"Okay," I said. I lifted the receiver. "Hello?" Silence.

"Hello?" I said again, just in case it was Dad trying to get through long distance or something.

I heard the sound of breathing. "Are you alone?" the voice asked huskily.

"No! No, I am not alone, okay?" I slammed down the receiver.

"Who was it?" Mike asked.

"Wrong number," I said shakily. I hadn't told anyone about the calls. They'd started a couple of weeks earlier, and I'd been afraid that if I'd said something, Dad and Leigh would have found a baby-sitter to stay with us while they were on their trip or worse, that they'd have canceled the honeymoon. The calls were scary, but harmless—though Leigh would never have seen them that way.

"Just a wrong number," I said again.

A few minutes later, David and Martha arrived with the pizzas. David kissed me quickly, then rushed the pizzas into the kitchen so we could keep them warm in the oven. Courtenay was starving and couldn't wait to have her piece, so we settled her at the table with a lukewarm slice, a Coke, and a roll of paper towels.

The doorbell rang again and I answered it fast. I was pretty hungry myself. Standing on our doorstep were Jane and Andrew—and Brad. I felt my stomach drop.

Brad was too old to be hanging around with us. He was twenty-one and should have been in college, where twenty-one-year-olds belong. But he dropped out during the second semester of his freshman year and never went back. He became a busboy at P.J.'s

Pancake House on Nassau Street. The rest of the time, he hung around his house.

He gave everyone the creeps.

He would ask me weird questions, he'd never smile, he'd sit too close to me, and he'd always have his hand on my arm or leg or someplace when he talked to me. The one thing he's got going for him is that he's *incredibly* handsome. Jane and Andrew have this odd coloring—olive skin with light brown hair, so that, especially during the summer when they're tan, they look all one color. But Brad has olive skin with jet-black hair, like Raul Julia, the actor. His eyes are piercing and dark and almost (but not quite) too large for his face. And his eyebrows are as expressive as a puppy's. All he has to do is move them a fraction of an inch and he can go from happy to worried to evil.

Personally, I think it's a shame to waste such good looks on such a weird person. Andrew and Jane are so nice, but while they're not bad-looking, they're just not great-looking.

Jane, Andrew, and Brad came in, and everybody began talking at once.

"I'm starved."

"The pizzas are here."

"Where's Courtenay?"

"Guess what's on TV tonight?"

"Hi, baby." (That was Brad, of course.) He came in and slipped his arm around me before I had even closed the door all the way.

I ducked out from under him and made a face at Jane that said, "Why did you bring *him* along?"

Jane shrugged sheepishly. She knew how I felt about Brad. She didn't like him much herself. When she was little, he teased her mercilessly, even though he was six years older than she. And some of his teasing wasn't harmless. He used to blackmail her, just like he blackmailed everyone else, and forced her to lie to their parents. Once, when she was seven, he stole her underwear after a summer swimming class, and Jane had to walk home with nothing on under her sundress. All the kids knew it and the boys kept lifting her dress to see what was (or wasn't) beneath. I truly believed that Brad was one of the reasons I was not as close to Jane as I was to Martha. I'd do anything not to be near him.

Jane pulled me into the den and shut the door partway. "I'm sorry," she whispered. "Andrew and I tried to get out without him, but he knew where we were going. He insisted on coming with us. He said he'd tell Mom and Dad about the F Andrew got on the history test last week if we didn't let him come. It was bizarre. I mean, it was bizarre that he wanted to come so badly, not that he was tormenting Andrew again."

I sighed. "Maybe we can get rid of him."

"If only he were a dog," said Jane. "We could toss a scrap of meat out the front door, and he'd run after it."

I giggled.

"Okay. I guess we'll just have to put up with him."

But I wasn't sure how long I could do that, especially when I walked out of the den and into the kitchen to find Brad holding Courtenay on his lap, bouncing her up and down. What I didn't like was the way he was touching her, but what I said was, "Brad, put her down, okay? She just ate. You'll upset her stomach if you jiggle her around."

"Sure, baby."

I drew in my breath. "My name is Maggie. Feel free to call me that. Everyone else does."

"Even David?"

I frowned. "Of course David. What did you think?"

Brad grinned. "Cool out, ba— Maggie. We can have a lovely evening together if you just relax."

I glanced at David, who shrugged.

I told you Brad was slime.

For the next hour, Brad divided his attention between Courtie and me. I could tell that Jane and Martha were both relieved and disgusted. They were relieved that Brad wasn't bothering them, and they were disgusted because he was bothering us. With Brad, you couldn't win. I kept throwing pointed looks to David and my brother, and they kept trying to distract Brad, but neither of them actually said much to him. They knew better. If they had done anything, Brad would have gotten back at them somehow. In fact, the things I said about calling me by my name were pretty risky. Brad was probably going to get me for something soon. I shivered at the thought. We'd all tangled with him at one time or another, and believe me, it wasn't pleasant.

After we had brought the pizzas out and settled down to our feast, David and I grabbed a moment alone together. I made sure that Courtenay was under Mike's watchful eyes. Then I said, "David, help me in the kitchen for a sec, okay?"

"Sure," he replied.

We headed for the kitchen.

David is big. That's about the best way I can describe him. He's big physically, well over six feet tall (he plays on the varsity football team), and he's big-hearted. He'll do just about anything for anyone. But he's not a pushover. He's like a huge, kind bear. And while he knows how to have fun (he and Mike are always kidding around), he's serious about school. He's preparing very carefully for college, because after that he wants to go to law school.

I can't think much past tomorrow, let alone past *college*.

"What's up?" asked David as the kitchen door swung shut behind us.

"Nothing. I just wanted to see you alone for a few minutes. It's weird, but I feel funny getting close to you when Brad's around. I don't know why."

"No. It's all right. I know what you mean. I feel funny, too."

"Well, let's forget about him for a while."

David folded me into his arms and simply held me for a long, long minute.

Then we heard Brad say from the other room, "What could they possibly be doing?"

I pulled away from David. We smiled at each other.

"We better get back out there," I said. "Here, let's bring a bottle of Coke with us so it looks like we were doing something."

"We *were* doing something."

I grinned. "You know what I mean."

We returned to the party.

Around eight when Brad grabbed Courtenay out of my lap and said, "Let's play horsey, honey," I stood up and said casually, "Gosh, Court, it's past your bedtime. Let's go upstairs." I grabbed her back from Brad. It wasn't past Courtenay's bedtime at all, but she was tired from the evening, and couldn't tell time anyway, so she didn't know the difference. "I'll be back in a while," I said to everyone.

Upstairs, I helped Courtenay wash her face and brush her teeth. She put on her Cabbage Patch Kids nightgown by herself, and we settled down on her bed with *Ramona the Pest*, which Leigh and I were reading to her a little each night. I flipped ahead and realized we would probably finish the book before Dad and Leigh came back from Saint Bart's.

At one point, while Courtenay was laughing over something Ramona said, I could have sworn I heard a creak in the hallway just outside the bedroom. A footstep?

"Shh a minute, Courtie," I said, and she did, but all I could hear were the TV downstairs and the faraway murmur of voices. I began reading again.

When Courtenay was asleep, I went back downstairs to find that Brad had left.

Jane grinned at me.

"Where is he?" I asked.

"Who cares?" she replied. "He's not here!"

For some reason, that didn't make me feel any better. Three times that evening I went upstairs to check on Courtenay, even though she wasn't crying or calling out. And each time she was fine.

A feeling of unease had settled over me.

4

Missing

The uneasiness disappeared by the time I woke up the next morning. And we had so much fun taking Courtie to the park on that beautiful day that none of us wanted to go back to school. But Monday morning arrived, and with it rain, and we were thrust back into our routine.

I was in charge of breakfast that morning, so Mike dressed Courtenay while I tried to come up with something more interesting than toast. I was overjoyed to find a stack of frozen breakfasts in the freezer. I popped three in the oven.

When we were ready to eat, I made Mike and Courtenay sit at the table while I served them.

"The lady is a magician, folks," said Mike, eyeing the stove suspiciously. "I don't see any pots and pans."

"Close your eyes," I said. I removed the breakfasts

from the oven, dumped everything out of the foil trays, and arranged the food on three plates.

Then I set the plates on the table and sat down. "Okay, open your eyes."

"Hey!" said Mike in surprise. "Where did this come from?"

I giggled and held up the empty boxes and trays. "Swanson's," I said.

Mike burst out laughing, but Courtenay didn't know what was so funny. She didn't care, either. She was just happy to be eating waffles on a gray Monday morning. And she was a big mess by the time she finished, with syrup everywhere, including in her hair. But we got her cleaned up and ready for school in time to greet Birdie, who was driving again that morning.

Courtie dashed down the front walk to her bus. "Hi, Birdie! Hi, Birdie-Birdie!" She was in high spirits. Waffles and Birdie. A good start to her day.

"Hi there, young lady."

I approached the bus, carrying Courtenay's lunch, which she'd forgotten in her excitement. "Morning, Birdie." I handed the lunch into the bus.

"Morning, Missy." "Missy" is what Birdie calls any girl whose name she can't remember. "Great day!"

I glanced at the sky. It was growing darker by the minute. "I guess..." I replied.

"A great day for me. I'm getting my hair done. Right after I drop off the kiddies. Maybe I'll try a new shade."

"Oh, have fun!" I called as Birdie put the bus in reverse and backed down the driveway. I waved to Courtenay and she waved back, her nose pressed against the window.

Mike was supposed to be the one to go home after school that day and wait for Courtenay. David and I had plans to walk to the public library and look for books for a history paper. But Mike caught up with me during my free period, looking half harried and half angry, and said, "Maggie, I don't believe it. Fiske is making me stay after school today." Fiske is Mike's math teacher. He's about a hundred years old.

"*You?* Why?" Mike never gets in trouble. And math is his best subject.

"He says I didn't turn in my quiz paper last Friday. What he means is he can't find it. He's *senile*. So he's making me stay this afternoon to take the quiz again. He practically accused me of cheating."

"Boy, if only Dad were here," I said.

"Yeah, well. I can handle it. But it means I can't wait for Courtenay. Can you do it?"

"Sure," I said, but I was really disappointed. Even a study date with David was pretty exciting.

"Thanks," said Mike. "I'll meet her the next two days."

"Okay." And that was how I happened to be the one sitting out on our damp front steps that afternoon waiting for Courtie's bus.

When I first sat down, it was about two-fifty, a little early for the bus, which usually arrived at three, so I got up, went into the kitchen, and made Courtenay a pitcher of apple and grape juice with pieces of apple floating in it. We call this Courtie's Punch, and she loves it. Leigh says it's a good way to get some fruit in her.

Then I took my French book and sat down on the porch steps with it. I was having a very hard time understanding this verb tense called the subjunctive. I just couldn't figure out when to use it, and I knew I'd have to understand it in order to do well on the French final exam. I studied the chapter. At last something began to make sense. What a relief. Maybe I'd get it figured out after all.

I looked at my watch. It read 3:05. The bus was late. That never happened. What could have gone wrong? A flat tire? An *accident?* I wondered who was driving. Probably not Birdie, since she'd driven two times in a row.

Don't panic, I told myself. I sat on the steps and decided to wait five more minutes before I did anything. I opened my French book to the back and took a self-quiz on the subjunctive. I answered all but two questions correctly. What an improvement.

Okay. It was time to take action. Courtie's bus was definitely late. I thought for a moment. Jennifer McLogan, Jane's cousin, also goes to Courtie's school. She was usually dropped off just before Courtie was. I decided to start by calling the McLogans to see whether Jennifer had arrived home yet.

I checked the list of phone numbers by the kitchen

telephone, found the McLogans', and dialed it.

"Hello?" a voice answered.

"Jane?" I asked hesitantly.

"Yeah.... Maggie?"

"Yeah. What are you... Didn't I dial the McLogans'?"

"Yup. I'm baby-sitting for Jenny and Scott this afternoon."

"Oh," I said. "Well, listen. Is Jenny home from school yet? Did the bus drop her off?"

"Yes. Right on time. Why?"

"You're kidding." Panic was rising in me, but I fought it back. There was no reason to panic yet. Anything could have happened. A flat tire. A traffic jam. A tree in the road. One of the kids had an upset stomach.

I twisted the phone cord around and looked out the kitchen window. The sky had been gray all day, but now it seemed threatening. It hung heavy and black and the air had grown very still. There was not a breath of wind. As I watched, a flash of lightning streaked through the sky above the tops of the poplar trees, which were the color of charcoal in the eerie light.

I shivered and turned away from the window.

"Why?" I repeated Jane's question. "Because Courtenay's not home yet."

"She's *not?*" Jane sounded slightly alarmed.

"No. I—I guess I should call the school. If the bus is in trouble somewhere, the school would know about it. The other parents must be worried, too."

I got off the phone with Jane. I was just about to call Courtenay's school when something occurred to me. Maybe somehow Courtenay had been let off the bus early. Maybe the route had changed. Courtenay could have gotten home before I did!

I made a fast search of the house, even though it would have been locked when Courtie got home and she wouldn't have been able to let herself in. No Courtenay.

Then I called several of our neighbors. No Courtenay.

I called the home of Courtie's good friend Gabbie Perkins, who also rode the bus, to see if possibly, just possibly, Courtenay had gone home with her at the last minute. But I knew perfectly well that in the first place, Mrs. Perkins would have called to let us know where Courtie was, and in the second place, the bus driver wouldn't have allowed it and neither would the school. A child needed written permission to go to any destination other than his or her home. I called the Perkinses anyway. No Courtenay.

Finally I called the school. The woman who answered the phone said she was the school secretary. I introduced myself and explained my problem to her.

"Well," she replied, "we haven't had a report that anything happened to the bus. Mr. Gunderson was driving this afternoon. Let me find out whether he's finished with his route. I'll call you right back, okay, Maggie? I'm sure there's nothing to worry about."

I was glad she said that. I needed to be reassured.

I sat on a chair by the phone with my hand on the

receiver. In a couple of minutes, the phone jangled, making me jump. I grabbed it.

"Hello?"

"Hi, Maggie." It was the school secretary. "I just spoke to Mr. Gunderson. He said Courtenay wasn't on the bus this afternoon."

"Not on the bus! I don't believe it. Can—can you hold on a minute?"

I abandoned the phone in the kitchen and ran up to Leigh's studio, where she has a private business line. I called Jane again. "Jane," I said, trying not to sound *too* nervous. "Could you please ask Jenny if Courtie was on the bus this afternoon? It's really important." I figured Jenny would know since there were only eight kids on the route.

"Sure. Hold on." There was a pause. Then Jane got on the phone again and said breathlessly, "Jenny said no—she wasn't."

"Oh—" I cried.

"Maggie, what's going on?" asked Jane, but I didn't bother to answer her. I simply hung up the phone.

Back in the kitchen, I spoke with the secretary again. "She really wasn't on the bus!" I exclaimed. "Where could she be?"

"Maggie," the secretary said quietly, "I checked with Courtenay's teacher while I waited for you... Courtenay wasn't in school today."

Wasn't in school? "But I saw her get on the bus this morning."

"All right," said the secretary. "I've got some calls

to make and some more checking to do. Sit tight for ten minutes, and I'll call you back."

Once again I hung up the phone. The school, I knew, was liable for Courtenay if she'd been on the bus. They'd want to talk to Birdie and maybe a couple of parents along the route.

I waited, not for ten minutes but for an eternity. At last the phone rang. I snatched up the receiver. The principal of the school was on the phone. "According to Birdie," she said, "Courtenay got off the bus when it reached school. Somehow, though, she never made it inside. It's time to call the police, Maggie. I want you to know that we'll help you every step of the way."

I didn't bother to hang up the phone again. I simply depressed the button, waited for the dial tone, and called the police.

5

Questions

The police were very nice, considering I sounded hysterical on the phone. They asked a million questions. What was Courtenay's hair color, skin color, her height, her weight? What was she wearing? Did she have any unusual mannerisms? Where was she last seen? I answered their questions as carefully as possible. They said they'd send a couple of officers over to the house immediately. I hung up the phone, slumped into the kitchen chair, put my hands over my eyes—and found that I couldn't cry. I tried to call Dad and Leigh then. It had to be done. But I couldn't reach them. The overseas operator said she'd call back.

A minute later, the phone rang.

"Hello? Hello?" I said. I listened for static. The connection with the operator had been very poor. But I heard only light breathing.

Something occurred to me—a wonderful possibility: "Courtenay?...Courtie, is that you?" I cried. I was immensely grateful to Mike and myself for having taught her to use the phone. "This is Maggie," I continued. "Where are you? Are you looking for a policeman?"

The voice on the other end of the phone laughed deeply. There was a pause. Then it asked, "Are you there alone?"

"No!" I screamed. "No!" I slammed the receiver into the cradle. What to do next? Mike. I should get Mike. I called Princeton High and got another school secretary.

"Can you please find Michael Ellis?" My voice was high and wavery. "He's probably with Mr. Fiske. This is an emergency!...What? Oh, this is his sister, Maggie. Please, can you find him? In fact, just tell him to come home. Our sister is missing."

As soon as I got off the phone, it rang again. I didn't know what to do. I was sure it was the caller. But it could be Mike or the police or the operator or Courtie's school or even Courtie. I stood in the kitchen hesitating, my heart hammering, remembering the caller's raspy breathing, his constant question: "Are you alone?" What if one day I replied, "Sure, I am. Come on over!"?

After three rings the phone was silent. I didn't have to decide whether to answer it. I only hoped it was a wrong number and not Courtenay. I sat down in the living room briefly, drumming my fingers on the arms

of a chair. Oh, Leigh was going to kill me. *Kill* me. I'd
failed her as completely as it was possible to fail a
person. I wondered if she could disclaim me as her
stepdaughter.

The emptiness of our big house surrounded me, en-
veloped me.... *C-R-E-A-K*. What was that? I glanced
fearfully around the room, not wanting to know what
the creak was, yet desperately needing to know it was
nothing. The room was dim. The day was darker than
ever, and I hadn't turned on any lights yet. I ran
around, switched on every lamp on the first floor,
locked all the windows and all the doors, and then
decided I was still too afraid to stay in the house
alone. I let myself out the front door and stood on the
steps shivering, watching the storm grow angrier.

The wind blew the tops of the trees violently back
and forth. Lightning flashed almost continually. In
the distance thunder rumbled, but no rain fell. Poor
Courtenay, I thought. Was she out in this? She was
afraid of thunder, almost as afraid of it as she was of
the red mitten that snores.

Less than ten minutes after I'd called the police,
Mike, two officers, and the rain all arrived, and all
arrived fast. Mike came charging up the street and
across the lawn just as a squad car pulled to a stop by
our mailbox and two police officers stepped out and
started across the lawn. Before any of them reached
the porch, the sky let loose and the rain pelted down
in huge drops that stung when they touched our skin.

I held the front door open.

"Maggie, what's wrong? What's going on?" Mike asked.

The police officers followed us into the house. They were two young men who didn't look much older than Mike. "I'm Officer Stuart," said one, a thin man with a scraggly mustache, "and this is Officer Martinez." He pointed to his partner, a dark-skinned guy with friendly eyes.

We stood in the front hall. Mike looked totally confused.

"I'm Maggie Ellis," I said, swallowing hard and trying to control my breathing. "This is my brother, Mike. He just got home." I turned to Mike. "Courtenay is missing," I explained. "She didn't come home this afternoon, so I called the school, and the secretary said she wasn't *in* school today."

"Wasn't in *school?*" exclaimed Mike. "But what happened after she got on the bus?"

"Well, that's what we're here to find out," said Martinez. "You'll need to file a missing-person report and we'd like to ask you some questions. Can we sit down?"

"Sure," I replied. I hung up their wet coats and showed them into the living room.

I sat down nervously next to Mike on the couch. The officers sat opposite us in armchairs.

"Now," said Martinez, "let's start at the beginning. Your sister's name is—?"

"Courtenay," Mike supplied. He spelled it out. "Courtenay Louise Ellis."

"And she's how old?"

"Four."

"When's her birthday?"

"July fifteenth. She'll be five in July."

Martinez nodded. "Do you have a recent photograph of her?"

"Tons," Mike said.

I gave Martinez Courtenay's school picture from the previous autumn while Mike got one of our photo albums. Martinez continued with the questions. "Where are your parents?" he asked.

"On vacation. Down in Saint Bart's."

Martinez frowned.

"Saint Barthélemy," I explained. "It's an island in the West Indies."

"Have you tried to reach them?"

"Yes, but I couldn't get through. I'm waiting for the operator to call back."

"Good," said Martinez. "Any other kids in your family?"

"No. Just us. Courtenay's actually our half sister."

"Your half sister," repeated Martinez. "So one of your parents is a stepparent?"

"Yes. Dad is our natural father, Mike's and mine. Leigh is our stepmother. Courtenay is Dad and Leigh's kid."

"And where is your mother?"

"Mine? I'm not sure. California, probably, but I don't know where. The last address I was writing to was in Michigan, but she's moved since then. She's one of those people who can't settle down. We haven't seen her since she left."

"How long ago was that?"

"Look, I don't mean to be rude," I said suddenly, "but shouldn't you be searching for Courtenay?"

Officer Stewart smiled. "It's okay. I know you're worried and upset. The police have already been alerted. They can do even more when they have your sister's photo. And believe me, these questions are important."

The doorbell rang then, and Officer Martinez rose to answer it while Mike came in with three photos of Courtenay. One of the pictures had been taken just two weeks earlier.

"Good," said Martinez when he saw the photos. He kept the school photo, gave the others to a policeman who was standing, dripping, in the front doorway, and sent the officer back out in the rain.

"Now the search can really get under way," Stewart said. "But we've got to continue the questioning. It's very important. I don't want to scare you, but when a child disappears, there's a better chance that she ran away or was kidnapped than that she's lost. And the kidnapper may be known to the victim. That's why we need all this information. We have to put the pieces together so we can make a priority statement, determine the status of the case."

I sat on the couch, frozen. Kidnapped. Had he really said that? I was thinking Courtie had just wandered off. Or I was hoping it, I guess. But underneath

I had known of the possibility of kidnapping. Wasn't that partly what the Lost Game was all about? Stay away from strangers, don't get into a car with someone you don't know. Want some candy, little girl?

Martinez picked up where he had left off. "Okay. Your parents are divorced. For how long?"

"About eight years," answered Mike. I was glad to let him take over for a while.

"Maggie said your mother may be in California?"

"Maybe. Maggie's last card was postmarked Los Angeles, but we never know where she's going to be, just that she won't be with us. Oh," Mike added hastily, "not that she doesn't love us. She really does. She just needs plenty of freedom. She's sort of an... an old hippie, I guess you could say."

Martinez was still writing our answers on a pad of paper, but he was becoming less formal. "Divorce is tough," he commented. "It must be hard to be separated from your mother, especially if you never see her."

"Well," I said, "it is, I guess. I wish she'd visit us just once in a while. But she's not like that. She wasn't meant to be tied down to a family. She doesn't like convention. Besides, I think she'd feel uncomfortable now that Leigh and Courtenay are part of our family. It's like, where would she fit in? She never asks about Leigh and Courtenay. But Mike and I do hear from her pretty often. She sends lots of postcards. And I write to her whenever we have an address."

"Well, that's something, I guess. Could I see the card from Los Angeles, please?"

I retrieved it from my desk drawer. Martinez studied it. "I'd like to hold on to this," he said. "The FBI may need it." My eyeballs nearly dropped out of their sockets at the mention of the FBI, but Martinez went on, "This is your father's second marriage? What about Leigh, your stepmother?"

"You mean is it her second marriage, too?" asked Mike. "Uh, yes, it is, I think. Isn't it, Maggie?"

"Yeah. She was married once before she met our dad."

"Any children by that marriage?"

"No," I replied. "She told us about it once, remember, Mike? She was married to a man whose last name is Tierno. They wanted kids but couldn't have any together. I remember Leigh saying he was really angry when she had Courtenay. It was like he thought Courtenay should be his or something."

"Mr. Tierno felt that way?" Martinez was writing furiously, trying to get everything straight.

"Yeah."

"There's no chance Courtenay really *could* be his daughter, is there?" asked Stewart.

What a dirty question, I thought. I glanced at Mike and made a face. "Well," I said, "it wouldn't be very likely. Courtenay was born after Dad and Leigh had been married for a little over a year."

"Do you have any idea where this Mr. Tierno lives?" asked Martinez.

"Yes," I said slowly, trying to remember things I hadn't thought of in months. "Around here. Not in Princeton. Maybe in Lawrenceville."

"Can you remember his first name? Did you ever know it?"

Mike shook his head, but I said, "Wait! Yes, we do know it, Mike. He runs a bicycle repair shop. We went there once. It *is* in Lawrenceville. His name is Jack Tierno."

"Good girl," said Martinez. He nodded to Stewart. They exchanged a glance—almost as if they were talking with their eyes—and Stewart got up to use the phone in the kitchen.

"What?" said Mike anxiously.

"You think *Mr. Tierno* took Courtenay?" I exclaimed.

"It's a possibility," answered Martinez. "We have to check into it. Now let's get back to today. Tell me what happened this morning before you left for school, and this afternoon when you realized Courtenay was missing."

"Okay," I said. "Well, it was a pretty normal morning. I mean, we got up and Mike dressed Courtenay while I made breakfast."

"Anything unusual happen?"

Mike and I shook our heads.

"No phone calls or wrong numbers? *Any*thing out of the ordinary?"

"No," I replied.

"All right. And after breakfast?"

"We put Courtenay on the school bus. That was all. The driver was Birdie. She was glad to see Courtie. She always is. Today she was excited because she was going to have her hair done in the morning. She said she might dye it a new color."

Martinez raised his eyebrows. "So you actually watched your sister get on the school bus."

"Yes," I said firmly. "I watched her find a seat and sit down. As the bus backed down the driveway, she waved to me from the window."

"Has anyone gotten hold of this Birdie?" Martinez asked Stewart.

"Someone's questioning her now."

Martinez turned back to Mike and me. "We have to try to pinpoint when and where Courtenay disappeared. I can understand how the school let the day go by without notifying you that Courtenay was absent. Not every school has a policy of calling the child's home if he or she is out, to make sure something like this hasn't happened. What I don't understand is why the bus driver didn't notice that your sister wasn't on the bus in the afternoon. Someone should have realized she was missing before you did."

"But," said Mike, "the afternoon driver isn't the same as the morning driver. The driving is done on a volunteer basis—by retired people—and the school doesn't give any of them too many trips each week."

"Well, that explains that," said Stewart. "I'll have someone talk to a couple of the children who were on the bus with Courtenay in the morning. I guess those are our only questions for you now, kids."

"Right," said Martinez. "We're going to send over some detectives, though. And I think one of you better try to reach your parents again. Then, Mike, I'd like you to go to the station with Stewart to file a missing-person report."

Mike nodded grimly. "I'll call Dad," he said.

6

Bleak Tuesday

It took Mike a while to reach Dad. There's hardly any phone service on Saint Bart's, and to make things worse, it turned out that Dad and Leigh were not on Saint Bart's at all but had taken a boat back to Saint Martin for the day to visit friends. It was past dinnertime when Mike finally got through to them. By then, an awful lot of things had happened. Mike held a brief, quiet conversation with Dad that I did not overhear and did not want to overhear. Then he hung up. Dad and Leigh were going to leave Saint Bart's as fast as they could, of course, but they probably wouldn't arrive home before late the next afternoon.

Meanwhile, the search was underway. It had begun as soon as I'd called the police, but it really picked up after Martinez and Stewart finished questioning Mike and me. Everything happened so fast.

First of all, the police, satisfied that Dad and Leigh

actually were in Saint Bart's (ruling out what Sewart called a "parental abduction"), and having also ruled out the possibility that Courtenay had run away, determined the case a "stranger abduction." When Officer Stewart took Mike back to the police station to file a missing-person report, he also entered Courtenay's description in the FBI's National Crime Information Center computer. The computer would match information about Courtie's case with information and leads in every state in the country. At the same time, a special phone line at the police station was set up for Courtenay's case, so that any calls about her or the abduction could be coordinated with all the other search efforts.

Meanwhile, two detectives stationed themselves at our house to continue the case. One, Lamberton, was a heavyset man with thinning hair and a constant craving for coffee. The other was a woman, Becker, whom I liked very much. She had a no-nonsense attitude, yet seemed to understand how Mike and I were feeling.

Detective Becker gave me the phone number of an agency called Search for the Children that helps families locate missing children. It was after six o'clock by the time I called, but I reached their answering service, and a concerned woman took down some information about the case and told me that I would be contacted the next morning.

Meanwhile, an actual search was in progress in Princeton. Jane had called back while Mike and I were talking to the police officers in the afternoon. I briefly explained to her what was going on, and that was all it took to involve our neighbors, the kids at Princeton High, the members of the Kiwanis Club, and several other organizations in a massive search. The word had spread like wildfire, and before I knew it, our friends (and a lot of people we didn't know at all) were working with the police, combing the town. They formed human chains and searched every inch of wooded and open areas both in and around Princeton. I joined them for a while, working silently alongside David and Martha, but returned home after an hour, unable to bear being away from the phone. The search continued far into the night.

The police used specially trained dogs to help them search construction sites. They sent men down wells and storm drains. They looked for open septic tanks. None of the search efforts turned up a scrap of evidence of Courtenay, but no one was willing to give up.

The eleven o'clock news surprised me. I was watching it with Mike. (Detective Lamberton was at our house, but he was in the kitchen on the phone.) One of the first stories that night was about Courtenay. They flashed her picture on the screen, gave the details of the kidnapping, then showed her picture again and, under it, the date she had disappeared and the phone number that had been set up for people to call if they knew anything about her or her whereabouts.

"How did the news station find out so fast?" I asked Mike.

Lamberton appeared in the doorway to the den. "AP," he replied.

"What?"

"The Associated Press. They pick up stories like this in a flash. And believe me, it's the best thing that can happen."

"Why?" asked Mike.

"Because publicity is just what we need. The more people who know that Courtenay's missing and know what she looks like, the better the chances for her recovery. We encourage it. If you tuned into WHWH, you'd find Courtenay all over the local news. The papers will run stories tomorrow. They've been picking up information at the station. Undoubtedly, someone will want to interview you soon."

My head was spinning.

Late that night I awoke drenched with sweat after another nightmare. I sat up, breathing deeply, and reached for the light switch. Where was Courtie then? Was she asleep? Was she dreaming about the red mitten that snores? Who would comfort her when she woke up?

I looked at my clock. Two-thirty. I had a feeling it was going to be a very long night. And it was. I never really did go back to sleep. Finally, at six-fifteen I crept down the hall. Mike apparently was still in bed. At any rate, his door was closed.

I tiptoed downstairs. Lamberton and Becker, wear-

ing the same clothes they'd had on the day before,
were sitting at the kitchen table. They had decided to
spend the night. I was grateful. I felt much safer with
the detectives there. A huge pot of coffee had been
made, and a mugful of it sat before each one of them.

"Morning," said Becker.

"Any word yet?" I greeted them.

"Nothing concrete," replied Lamberton.

"What's that mean?"

"We have a lot of pieces to the puzzle and a few
clues, but we don't know how to fit everything together. The searchers knocked off around midnight
last night and are just about ready to begin again.
They haven't turned anything up, though."

"What kinds of clues do you have?" I asked. I
poured myself a cup of coffee and sat down at the
table with them.

"Don't get your hopes up," said Becker.

"I'll try not to."

"Someone spotted an unusual car, an old green
Ford," said Lamberton. "It was near the school at
about the time your sister's bus should have been ar-
riving. It might mean something, it might not."

I nodded. "What else?"

"Only one other important thing. Your stepmother's
first husband, Jack Tierno, seems to have conve-
niently gone out of town yesterday morning."

I thought that over. Then I asked, "Has anyone
seen Courtenay?"

"Oh, there have been a number of calls from people who say they've spotted a girl matching Cour-

tenay's description. One man said he spotted her in the Los Angeles airport at seven o'clock yesterday morning." Lamberton smiled ruefully. "Everyone thinks they've seen your sister. By the way, how would you and Mike feel about doing a TV interview sometime today? Ordinarily, we'd want your parents on the show, too, but I don't want to wait until they come home."

"It's very important," Becker said. "It shows people the purely personal, human-interest side of the case. They feel involved that way—and then they're more apt to report anything they might know or have seen. You could do the interview right here—in your living room, if you like."

"I'll talk to Mike," I said. "What happened when Birdie was questioned yesterday?"

"Well, she doesn't know much," Lamberton answered. "She finished the route. She knows that no kid got off the bus before she reached the school, unless the kid went out a window. In fact, she specifically remembers saying goodbye to your sister because Courtenay was the last kid off the bus and she blew Birdie a kiss as she went down the steps."

I smiled. "So she reached school," I said, trying to reconstruct everything.

"She reached school," said Lamberton. "And Birdie drove off. She didn't want to be late for her appointment with the hairdresser. So she didn't actually see Courtenay go into school."

"But it's not a long walk from the bus to the front door," I said. "And Courtenay's done it lots of times

—all year. What could have happened between getting off the bus and reaching the door? There are usually teachers around."

"That's what we're trying to figure out," said Becker. "There are a lot of ifs. For one thing, we only have Birdie's word that this is what happened. The other children back her up, basically, but they're only three and four years old."

"You mean you think Birdie's lying?"

"Who knows? No teacher remembers seeing Courtenay outside school."

I shuddered. "Birdie's always been sorry she didn't have kids of her own. She told me so once. That's why she likes driving the bus."

Lamberton nodded as if he already knew that.

I began to feel sick.

The phone jangled noisily just as I was rising from the table.

"Do you want to answer it?" asked Becker.

"Okay," I said. I picked it up. "Hello?"

"Hi, Maggie." It was Martha. "Sorry to call so early, but I figured you'd be up. I just wanted to see how you're doing. I'm going to help search again today. Mr. Sakala is giving two days off to any student who wants to join in the search." (Mr. Sakala is the principal of Princeton High.)

"Wow, that's really nice of him," I said.

"Are you going to help again today?"

"I don't know. Probably not. Dad and Leigh are coming home, and the police want Mike and me to do a TV interview."

"Well, is it okay if I come over this afternoon? I'd like to see you."

"I guess it's okay," I replied. "It will depend a little on when Dad and Leigh get home."

"Oh, I understand," said Martha.

"I better get off. I don't want to tie up the phone in case anyone's trying to call about Courtenay."

"Okay. See you this afternoon."

"'Bye."

When I hung up, I decided to go rouse Mike and tell him about the TV interview. I knocked softly on the closed door to his room. No answer. I knocked again. Still no answer. Slowly, I opened the door and peeked in. The bed was made, the shades were up, the room was as neat as a pin. It looked as if Mike hadn't slept there.

My heart began to pound wildly. What had Mike and I done last night? We'd watched the news. Then I'd gone to bed and—what had Mike done? Where had he gone?

I dashed downstairs, about to tell Lamberton that there was a second disappearance, then decided to check the house first. And in the den, the shades drawn, the lights off, I found Mike, just sitting and staring. He'd been there all night.

When I poked my head in, breathing a sigh of relief, he simply extended his hand to me. I walked over to him, took it, and we both sat on the couch and cried.

Five hours later, Dad and Leigh came home.

7

Secrets

Dad and Leigh walked into the kitchen at noon. Mike and I were there with the detectives, drinking coffee, waiting for the phone to ring. Mike had helped search for Courtenay for three hours that morning, but I felt afraid to leave the phone, sure that the moment I did, it would ring with the news that she had been found.

"Dad!" I cried, jumping up. "How'd you get home so early?" I ran to him and he put his arms around me.

"We rented a private plane in Saint Barts. I'll tell you the whole story some other time." He released me, greeted Mike, and turned to the detectives.

The introductions began.

I decided to brave the worst. I went to Leigh and helped her off with her raincoat. She accepted the help with stony silence.

"How are you?" I asked tentatively.

Leigh glared at me. "How do you think?" she said. And then, "How could you let this happen?" Each word was a shot like gunfire.

"It wasn't our fault," I protested. "Talk to the police. You'll see. We put Courtie on the school bus. She just never made it to school. It could have happened to any kid."

"But it happened to Courtie—while we were gone."

"Thanks to me, at least she knows what to do out there on her own."

Leigh started to say something, but Dad turned away from his discussion with Lamberton and Becker and waved us into silence. When the detectives had filled Dad and Leigh in on everything—the clues, the search, the investigation, what had happened the day before—Becker took Leigh into the den and Lamberton took Dad into the living room, and the questioning began. Becker closed the den door, so I don't know what went on in there, but I guessed that she was grilling Leigh about Jack Tierno. In the living room Lamberton went over the same stuff he had asked Mike and me.

Dad answered a couple of questions about Mom, sweating profusely even though the house was damp and slightly chilly from the rain.

"Why *are* you so interested in our mother?" I asked finally.

"It's not just your mother," Lamberton told me. "We're interested in Mr. Tierno, too. You see, if a missing child is of divorced parents, very often the abductor is one of the parents."

"But Courtenay's parents aren't divorced," I protested. "They're Dad and Leigh, and they're right here."

"We're simply considering all the angles," replied Lamberton, "and at the moment we have little to go on except the fact that Jack Tierno apparently was jealous that your father and stepmother could have a child when he and his wife were unable to.

"Now, Mr. Ellis," he continued, "I'd like some more details about your divorce and about the custody arrangements for Maggie and Mike. It's somewhat unusual for the father to be granted full custody."

Dad was starting to turn pale. I glanced at Mike. Mike was frowning.

"Maggie, Mike," said Dad. "Would you please leave the room?"

Lamberton looked sharply at my father.

"Why?" I asked.

"Just leave, please."

"No."

"Come on, Maggie," said Mike. "Let's go."

"No," I repeated more firmly. "If Dad has something to say about Mom or us, we ought to be allowed to hear it."

"I disagree," said Dad.

Lamberton began to look impatient. "Would you like to go down to the station for the questioning?"

My father appeared to consider the suggestion. But I cut in. "Dad, this is ridiculous. She's *our* mother. And Courtie is *our* sister. We have a right to know anything about them and this case."

For a long moment, my father sat unmoving, his head bowed. At last he said, "Maybe you're right, Maggie, but what you and Mike are going to hear is not going to be easy for you. There are things I've tried to keep from you. Someday, when the time was right, I might have told you the truth. Unfortunately, this is a terrible time and a terrible way for it to come out... If any of this is too difficult for you to handle, I—well, I'll have to answer the questions anyway. I'd still prefer that you not be here, but...". He trailed off.

At that moment, wild horses couldn't have dragged me away. I was consumed with curiosity.

"All right," said Lamberton, adjusting his heavy frame on the couch. "I'll go back over what I know already. Your wife left you eight years ago?"

"That's right."

"And she left voluntarily?"

"No."

No? "What do you mean, Dad?" I asked.

Dad looked at Lamberton, who nodded as if to say, "It's okay. Go ahead."

"The court asked her to leave," said my father. "She'd been charged with child abuse—neglecting and mentally abusing Maggie and Mike. When the divorce was final, I was given full custody. Jessica wasn't even allowed visitation rights."

I gasped. "That's not true!" I cried. "Our mother wouldn't hurt us. She had to leave because... because that's the way she is."

Dad couldn't look up. "I'm sorry," he said slowly, "but that's not so. That's the story I've told you and Mike, but it isn't true."

"You wouldn't lie to us, Dad," said Mike. I watched his stricken face. I could see the anger and fear and hurt, everything I was feeling. "You've taught us not to lie," he continued. "What are you covering up? Why are you lying now?"

"I'm not lying," my father repeated patiently. "I lied before. For all those years. I was trying to protect you and Maggie. I was hoping you wouldn't have to remember or understand the years with Jessica. I was trying to keep you from being hurt—again."

Before I could protest, Lamberton broke in and I listened numbly. "I'm afraid I'll have to ask you to describe the abuse, Mr. Ellis. How did your wife hurt the children?"

"Oh, it wasn't physical abuse," Dad replied quickly. "Jessica never raised a hand to the children. But in many ways she was a child herself, and she simply couldn't cope. When she needed peace, she'd leave the children and just take off, even when they were quite little. Maggie bore the brunt of the mental or emotional abuse, I'm afraid, although I don't know why. When Jessica became angry with Maggie, she would simply lock her in a closet and leave her there, sometimes for hours. If she felt particularly angry, she would hurt something belonging to Maggie, usually her dolls. That was one reason the psychiatrist who testified at the court hearings recommended that Jessica be separated from the children. He felt that Jessica's hurting the dolls represented what she *wished* she could do to Maggie. He said it was probably only a matter of time before that symbolic abuse became real."

I couldn't believe the words that were coming from my father's mouth. *Liar!* I wanted to shout.

Lamberton was writing away in his notebook. "Do you have any idea where your wife is now, Mr. Ellis?"

Dad shook his head. "None. I'd be surprised if she were still in L.A. She moves constantly, as Maggie and Mike told you."

"At least something was true," muttered Mike.

My father sighed. "She honestly is a free spirit, and really does drift from place to place, taking pottery classes or doing whatever strikes her fancy."

"Please think," Lamberton pressed Dad. "*Any* idea where she is?"

"I'm sorry. After the court decision, she's kept her distance from us. As far as I know she hasn't even returned to the Northeast. The postcards she sends come from California, Florida... For a while she was living somewhere in Canada, but that was several years ago."

"What the *hell* does all this have to do with Courtenay?" Mike exploded suddenly.

"It may have everything to do with her," said Lamberton sternly. "I'm sorry this is painful for you, but if you don't let me proceed with the questioning, you'll have to leave the room."

Mike slumped sullenly in his chair.

After a moment, Lamberton said, "Despite the denial of visitation rights, has Mrs. Ellis ever seen the children?"

"No," replied Dad.

"Has she ever tried to see them?"

My father paused and cleared his throat. "For the past ten months she's been trying to reverse the decision on the visitation rights. If she can do that, she hopes those rights will lead to shared custody of the children."

My mouth dropped open. "You never told us!" I accused him.

"I didn't see any need to. I'm fighting to deny all of her requests. There's no reason for you and Mike to get caught up in this mess."

A glare from Lamberton made me close my open mouth.

"Is Mrs. Ellis angry?" asked Lamberton.

"Very."

"Is she the kind of person who'd want revenge?"

"Yes."

"No," I whispered, but no one heard me.

"Could she have taken Courtenay?"

"I suppose so."

"*Dad!*"

"Maggie, shut *up*. Shut up right now." Dad stood

suddenly. He had never told anybody that I knew of to shut up. His face was beet red and he was boiling with anger. "For God's sake, this isn't any easier for me than it is for you. Do you think I've enjoyed living a lie? Do you think I've liked sneaking around and keeping secrets...and bursting your bubble about your wacky, beloved mother? This is no picnic. I loved your mother once, too." He sat down and addressed Lamberton. "I think this is farfetched. Jessica is unstable, but why would she take a child that doesn't belong to her?"

"Because of what Courtenay stands for," answered Lamberton quietly. "Your new life, your happy marriage, everything she couldn't have."

Dad nodded. "Yes, I see."

"Do you have any pictures of your ex-wife?"

"Only old ones. I haven't seen her since she left. She could have cut her hair, grown it, dyed it. She could look like an entirely different person."

Lamberton nodded tiredly. "But an old picture is better than nothing.

"Now," he went on, "I am going to ask all of you not to mention this to anyone—your friends or relatives, and especially not the press. Oh, you can tell your wife, of course," he said to Dad. "But it's imperative that we keep this angle absolutely private. For one thing, if the first Mrs. Ellis did take Courtenay, we don't want her to know we're on to her. If she thinks she's not a suspect, she may let her guard down. For another, there's the chance that Mrs. Ellis isn't involved at all, in which case we want the public to help search for Courtenay as they would any other missing child. However, Jessica Ellis is our prime suspect."

"You are crazy!" I screamed, leaping to my feet. "You and Dad both. My mother wouldn't do something like this, and I'm going to prove it." I ran up the stairs to my bedroom.

8

On the Air

A little while later, I tiptoed down the hall and sat at the top of the stairs, listening. Lamberton and Dad were still talking. I didn't know where Mike was.

"Are we doing everything we should be doing to locate Courtenay?" I heard my father ask.

Lamberton explained to Dad about the NCIC computer and the need for publicity.

I crept halfway down the stairs and looked at them through the railings of the banister. "There's one other thing, Dad," I said. He glanced up, surprised.

I told him about Search for the Children. "They called back this morning. I talked to them for a while, but they want to speak to you."

"Thank you, Maggie," he replied.

Dad contacted Search for the Children immediately. It was a national organization located in California. Dad called them on their toll-free number and talked to the woman I had spoken with that morning. They talked for a long time. The organization would help us distribute photos of Courtenay—on posters and milk cartons—nationwide. Work would begin right away, although the photos themselves could not actually go out for several weeks. The woman gave us tips on conducting our own search for Courtenay. She said that Search for the Children would work directly with the police and the FBI, on Courtie's case.

When Dad got off the phone, he looked haggard.

I retreated to my room.

At four-thirty that afternoon, Mike came into my room. "The TV crew is downstairs," he said, "and the detectives are done with Dad and Leigh. They want us all to go on the news show."

"Now?" I asked.

Mike nodded. "Stay tuned for the Leigh Ellis Show," he said wryly.

I didn't attempt a smile. "I don't really even want to be near Dad," I said.

"Maggie, I think that for the sake of the search we're going to have to put some of our feelings aside. If you want to prove that Mom didn't take Courtenay, then we have to do everything possible to get Courtie back—so Dad and the police can see who *did* take her, that it wasn't Mom. And that means a regular all-out search, which the police seem to want anyway."

"I guess."

"Come on. I know you can do it. And remember, we're not supposed to say anything about Mom."

"I know. Okay. Give me five minutes to get myself together."

The camera crew was setting up in the living room when I started downstairs in the old jeans and flannel shirt I'd been wearing. When I saw the crew, I went back upstairs, changed into new jeans and a sweater, and went down again.

Our living room looked like a real TV studio. A makeup woman fixed my face for the cameras and bright lights, clucking over my freckles and red hair. Later, two men posed Dad, Leigh, Mike and me on the couch, which wasn't at all easy, considering Leigh was mad at Mike and me, and Mike and I were mad at Dad, so nobody wanted to be near anybody else. The men tried us in nine different arrangements before they seemed satisfied.

At last the cameras began rolling. Robert Ford, anchorman for the Channel Three Eleven O'Clock Nightcast, interviewed each of us plus Lamberton and Becker. He asked Mike and me the most questions since we were the ones who had put Courtenay on the school bus. Then he stupidly said to Leigh, "And how does it feel to know your four-year-old is out there somewhere—frightened and confused?"

"How do you *think* it feels?" Leigh snapped. "It feels *won*derful. Wouldn't you be thrilled to pieces if *your* daughter were missing?" Then she began to cry, and when the camera zoomed in for a close-up of that novel sight, Leigh jerked her head up and said, "Turn that thing off! Don't you have any respect for a person's grief?"

I bet that none of that would be on the news that night.

I was right.

But a lot of the rest of the interview was on. As Becker had said earlier, it was important to capture for the public the personal, human-interest aspects of Courtenay's disappearance. She said this was because the more people who were aware of the disappearance and the more people who were out there keeping their eyes peeled for a little tawny-haired kid, the better the chances for Courtie's recovery. Becker also said that the best way to capture the public's interest was to make Courtie and our family as real as possible, and therefore as sympathetic as possible.

Which was how I ended up leading Robert Ford upstairs to Courtie's room, with a remote camera rolling away behind me the entire time. When we reached her room, Ford looked around, a fake expression of grimness on his face. The camera panned from side to side, taking in everything—Courtie's brass bed with the collection of dolls (Cabbage Patch, Raggedy Ann and Andy, Leigh's old Betsy Wetsy), her building blocks, the little bookcase overflowing with children's books that Dad had brought home from the office, the rocking chair, the desk with legs that looked like crayons.

Ford turned to me and the camera rolled on. "Tell me about your little sister," he said, overly earnestly. "What does she like to do? What kind of child is she?"

I thought for a moment. "Courtie is very smart," I

replied. "She likes to be read to. She likes to draw pictures."

"Here at her desk?" asked Ford, indicating the crayon table.

I nodded. "Yes. And even though she's very adult because she's around grownups so much, she has this great imagination. She likes to dress up in her mother's clothes. She's gotten married twice—without any groom." Ford smiled. "And she makes up long, wild stories. She also," I said, feeling a catch in my throat, "has nightmares. If you—if anybody out there has my sister right now, please help her if she cries at night." I began to cry myself. Of course the camera moved in. "She, um, thinks there's a red mitten under her bed that snores," I went on. "It scares her to death. You should know that."

Ford moved the microphone from my mouth to his. "A plea for a missing child," he said in his show-biz newscaster's voice. "Would you like to add anything to your statement, Maggie?"

I nodded into the camera, the tears still rolling down my cheeks. "Just please give her back safely," I whispered. "If you've taken my sister, please let us have her back. She belongs here in her room."

"Thank you, Maggie Ellis. This is Robert Ford, Channel Three News Nightcast."

The camera clicked off.

"That was beautiful, kid, beautiful."

I looked at Robert Ford and decided that both his hair and his tan were fake. Then I fled to my room, leaving him and the cameraman to find their own way downstairs. In my room, I stood at my window, gazing outside. The rain was clearing up slowly. I spotted the Channel Three van parked in our driveway and decided to wait until it left before I left my room.

As I stood looking, I realized that our house had become a curiosity. Most of our neighbors were still out searching, but other people kept driving by and slowing down for a glimpse of the home from which a child was missing.

Our street was a busy place. I also saw several newspaper reporters in the driveway behind the Channel Three van. I knew they'd been hanging around since the night before. Lamberton and Becker seemed pleased with this. They liked the publicity and would throw tidbits of information to the reporters every now and then.

The TV people began to leave our house, but it was taking them a while to load their equipment in the van. I settled into a more comfortable position, determined not to leave my room until that van was backing down our driveway. I saw Caroline and Sandra, two of Courtie's friends, playing in Caroline's front yard. I noticed that Mrs. Babbitt, Caroline's mother, was outdoors with them, watching them anxiously. I saw Martha walking by in a great hurry and wondered if she would come over.

It was just as Martha was walking past our mailbox that I spotted the figure in the trees. Across the street from us, at the corner of the Babbitts' front yard, is a

little stand of fir and ash trees. Our whole neighborhood was woods not too many years ago. In fact, it
was still pretty woodsy when Dad and Mike and I
moved from Herrontown Road after the divorce. As
the neighborhood grew, the only trees cut down were
those needed to clear space for the homes, so there
are a lot of trees around. The street is shady, the
houses almost secluded.

I jumped when I realized that the figure was Brad
de Christopher. What was he doing? Was he just another curious onlooker? As I stared out the window at
him, he casually shoved his hands in his pockets and
strode out from among the trees and down the sidewalk.

I shivered as fear ran its chilly fingers up my back.

9

Wednesday

Courtenay had been missing for two days. The police and searchers were turning up so few clues and having so little luck with people calling in about the case that they began to drag the lakes and rivers in the area. Then Lamberton told us about a child, a four-year-old boy, who was thought to have been kidnapped by his father after a messy divorce. Three days later, the boy's body was found in a refrigerator someone had left on the sidewalk for a secondhand store to cart away.

When Leigh heard that, she absolutely fell apart. Lamberton should have kept his mouth shut. Leigh wouldn't talk to anyone anyway, except sometimes Dad, and she wouldn't eat and she cried all the time.

Three interesting things happened on Wednesday, though. Mike and I had stayed home from school again, so we were in on everything. The first thing was that Lamberton and Becker, even with the river-dragging and stuff going on, sat Dad down after breakfast and brought up the remote possibility that Courtie had been kidnapped—not by Mom or even by someone who just wanted a kid, but by someone who wanted ransom money, like in the movies, or in that funny O. Henry story, "The Ransom of Red Chief." We hadn't received a ransom note or call, but Lamberton wanted to consider the possibility anyway.

"But I'm not that wealthy," said Dad. "I mean, we've got plenty of money, but I'm no millionaire."

"Doesn't necessarily matter," replied Lamberton. "Somebody might kidnap a child if he thought he'd get some money out of it. Would you pay, say, ten thousand dollars to have your daughter returned safely?"

"Of course."

"Well, there you are. Ten thousand dollars is a lot of money. It's not a million dollars, but it's a lot. Most people can get together *some* amount of money for the return of a child."

"How about offering a reward?" asked Dad. "Instead of waiting for the kidnapper to come to us, we'll go to him. I'd even pay Jessica to give us Courtenay back." I rolled my eyes, but Dad went on, "How about a reward of twenty-five thousand dollars?"

I gasped. That sounded like a fortune.

"It would certainly help," replied Becker, looking a bit surprised. "I'll let the papers know today. Or perhaps you'd like to have a news conference, Mr. Ellis. That might be more effective."

"All right," replied Dad quietly.

"What I'd also like to do," Lamberton went on, "is tell you—all of you—a few things about handling a phone call when someone says he or she has kidnapped Courtenay and wants the money in exchange for her return, which is bound to start happening after the reward is announced." Dad and Mike and I nodded. "There are a few dos and don'ts. We'd like to be able to weed out the people who have nothing to do with the case but simply want the money, so that we can pinpoint the actual kidnapper—if there is one, and if he or she should call."

We all nodded again.

"All right," said Lamberton. "If someone does say he or she has Courtenay, keep the person on the line for a while. We'll try to trace the call with this." He held up a small instrument, which he carefully attached to the phone in the kitchen. "If we can do that, then there's the chance—but it's a *small* chance—that we could find Courtenay before you have to meet anyone to hand over money. While you're talking, Detective Becker or I will use the other line upstairs to call the phone company. They'll be able to tell where the call is coming from."

"Okay," said Dad.

"It's not unreasonable to ask the caller for some sort of proof that he or she actually has Courtenay. It may indicate that the caller is a phony. The real kidnapper will expect you to want proof and will be eager to give it to you. Ask to speak to Courtenay or ask about ... Does Courtenay have any birthmarks or scars that the media *hasn't* mentioned but that the kidnapper would notice?"

Dad frowned.

"We mentioned her birthmark," I spoke up, "but Dad, remember when she fell on the patio last year?"

"Oh, that's right," said Dad. "She had two stitches taken just over her right eyebrow. It's a tiny little scar, but you can still see where the stitches were."

"Okay," said Lamberton. "Ask the caller to describe the scar on Courtenay's face. Don't give any more clues than that. If he can't do it, he doesn't really have her."

Lamberton talked until I couldn't follow him anymore. All I could think of was Courtie. I saw her waving from the bus window, crying about the red mitten, grinning with a mouthful of pizza. I tried to picture her with Mom, but that was too depressing. When Lamberton was finished, I went to my room and cried.

Late that afternoon, David came over. The kids who'd been searching for Courtenay had to return to school the next day. Most of them were exhausted and had already knocked off. I'd never been so glad to see someone.

When I answered the doorbell, David strode into the hall, wrapped his arms around me in one of his bear hugs, and held me, rocking me back and forth like a baby. Of course I began to cry again. Everyone who was around suddenly became busy with other things so that David and I could feel as if we were alone. After a few minutes, we sneaked into the den.

"I saw you on TV last night," David said.

I blushed. "What did you think?"

"That Robert Ford is a jerk. But you did a good job. You looked as if all you cared about is getting Courtenay back. You looked really pretty, too." David was holding one of my hands between both of his and stroking it with his thumb.

"Thanks," I whispered.

"What are the police turning up? Anything important since the last time I talked to you?"

I shook my head. "So far they've been questioning people, a lot of people. The state police are trying to get hold of Leigh's first husband, but they haven't been able to reach him. Courtie's teacher has been questioned but she doesn't know anything. Birdie's been questioned, too. I think they're a little suspicious of her."

"How well do you know Birdie?" asked David.

"I see her pretty often," I replied. "She was Courtie's favorite driver—I mean, *is* her favorite driver—and I used to like her a lot, too, but..."

"But what?"

"Well, I just don't know what to think. I've been going over this, and now all sorts of things seem funny to me, like the fact that Birdie was going to have her hair dyed. If she were planning to kidnap Courtie, she'd need a disguise for later—but then why would she tell me about her hair? Also, she's always said she wished she could have had a child. Maybe she wanted one so badly, she *took* one. Courtie was one of her favorite kids."

David looked thoughtful. "It could be important, it could be nothing."

"I know." I laid my head on his shoulder, and he turned to kiss my forehead.

The phone rang. I jumped a mile.

"Hey," said David softly, "it's okay."

"I want to see who's on the phone. Maybe it's the kidnapper."

We got to the kitchen just as Mike was putting the receiver back in the cradle.

"Who was it?" I asked. "Was it about Courtenay?"

Mike shook his head. "Wrong number, I guess. The person hung up as soon as I said hello."

"Oh."

Dad came into the kitchen with Leigh clutching his arm and sort of leaning against him. She looked terrible. She was still in her bathrobe. Her eyes were red from crying, and there were dark circles under them. Her face was as pale as a sheet. Without makeup, she looked positively ghoulish.

Dad guided her to the table and sat her down.

"Want some coffee, Leigh?" I asked her.

She shook her head and pressed her fingertips against her brow.

"Something to eat? I could make scrambled eggs..."

Leigh shook her head again.

"... or a grilled cheese sandwich."

"Maggie, *no*. I don't want anything. Just Courtenay. All I want is to have my baby back."

"Well, I'm afraid I can't provide that," I snapped, and stalked out of the kitchen.

David followed me. "Maggie?"

"I'm all right," I said. "Maybe you should go, though. Leigh's in an awful mood. But could Mike and I come over tonight?"

"Sure. That'd be fine."

"Good. See if Jane and Andrew—*but not Brad*— can come, too. I want to discuss something with everyone."

"All right. Are you going to tell me what this is all about?"

I smiled and shook my head.

He grinned. "I didn't think so, but I've got an idea about it. You know I'll do anything I can to help."

Of course he would. David Jacobssen couldn't *not* help someone who needed him.

"Listen, I'll call before we come over, but don't you call here," I said. "The fewer phone calls, the better."

David nodded. He pulled me into the den, closed the door, and kissed my lips softly—again and again. We pulled apart for a few seconds, and I drew in my breath sharply. He'd kissed me before, but never like *that*. Then we kissed tenderly once more, and without another word, David left the house.

10

Wednesday Night

Becker questioned Jack Tierno. She gave Dad and Mike and me the news shortly after David left. "The state police had staked out his house," she said. "As soon as he got back from his trip, I went over there to question him. He has an airtight alibi. He's been at some sort of bicycle convention in Minneapolis since Saturday. I've already checked him out. Dozens of people vouch for him. On Monday he attended meetings, a breakfast, and a lunch. There's no way he was even *near* Princeton."

So Jack Tierno was clean—but not out of the picture. He called our house twice wanting to talk to Leigh, telling her how sorry he was. I got the distinct impression that Jack wasn't the one who'd wanted that marriage to end, that he was still in love with Leigh, and that he was truly sorry she was hurting so. I felt bad for him. It was clear that despite whatever had happened, Leigh remained important to him.

"Any leads on Mom?" David asked Becker carefully.

"*David*," I said warningly.

"I have to know," he replied crossly. "Lay off, Maggie."

"Unfortunately, none," said Becker. "The FBI are trying to track her down, but they have nothing to go on aside from the postmark on her recent card to Maggie."

"Good," I said.

"I think that right now you should concentrate your efforts on publicizing Courtenay's disappearance," Becker said.

"Haven't we been doing that?" asked Mike.

"Yes, and the reward is a big help, but the more you can do, the better. The public has a short memory."

"I have a question," I spoke up. "On TV, when a kid is missing, the family and neighbors make up posters with a photo of the child on them and put them up all over the place—in stores, on phone poles, in bus stations and restaurants, anywhere a lot of people will see them. Search for the Children will do this sort of thing, but the photos won't be distributed for a while. Shouldn't we be putting up our own notices about Courtenay?"

"Of course. Everything helps. In fact, a group of your neighbors are already working on fliers to hand out. Posters would be terrific. But they must be distributed widely."

"Are you saying we shouldn't bother?" I asked.

"Not at all," Becker replied. "I'm saying that the more widely you can distribute the posters, the better. Get them all across the country, if possible."

Dad noticed the stricken look on my face. "Maggie?" he said gently. "What is it?"

"I was going to get all our friends together tonight so we could figure out how to print the posters, but we'll barely be able to get them up around Princeton, let alone the whole country."

"Oh, Maggie." Dad reached over and patted my knee. I pulled away from him and he sighed.

Instead of eating dinner that evening, I took a nap. When I woke up, I felt better. I wandered into Mike's room. He was sitting in the dark again, and scared me to death by calling out my name like some disembodied ghoul. "Mike!" I cried with a gasp. "Don't do that!"

"Sorry."

"Want to go over to David and Martha's?" I asked. "I decided that we should make up posters anyway, even if we can only make enough for our *street*. Every little bit helps."

There was a long pause. Courtenay was weighing heavily on all of us. "I thought I'd try to catch up on some of the work I've missed," he said.

"Oh, come on. You know you won't do any homework tonight. Besides, you were the one who said we have to conduct a regular search if we want to find out who took Courtenay. Wouldn't you just love to be able to present Dad with some weirdo, and say, 'Here's the person who took Courtie. Does he look like Mom to you?' Anyway, I already told David to ask Jane and Andrew over tonight. I'm going to call David now."

Silence.

"Okay?"

"Sure."

I backed out of Mike's room, feeling slightly afraid.

I made the call as short as possible. "David? It's me. Is it okay if we come over now?...Great. See you in a few minutes." I hung up the phone and went downstairs to find Becker. "Mike and I are going to go over to the Jacobssens' to see about printing up posters."

"Okay, hon," replied Becker. "Here." She handed me a poster with the picture of a young girl printed on it. "It's a typical poster. This girl is currently missing from Brooklyn, New York, and it contains all the information you should include on your poster. Okay?"

I nodded. "Thanks," I said, looking at the photo of the girl. Lacey Meigs was her name. She had jet-black hair and dark, laughing eyes. She had been missing for—I checked the poster again—fourteen months. "Over a year!" I exclaimed. "Gone for more than a *year?*"

Becker nodded. "I'm afraid that in the world of missing children, a year isn't very long. Lots of children have been missing for more than five years.

Most of them will never be found. Not after that much time has passed."

"*Lots* of children?" I repeated. "Just how many children are missing?"

"In the United States—thousands."

"*Thou*sands? But that's impossible! How could so many children be *miss*ing? Why don't we know about them? Where are they? Don't people talk about them? When an adult is kidnapped it makes national news, doesn't it? Why don't we hear about all these children?"

"Well," Becker began to explain, "about ninety percent of them are teenage runaways. The rest—"

The phone rang. I snatched it up.

"Hello?" I said harshly.

There was a pause. Then, "Are you there alone?" asked the familiar voice. "You're not, are you?" I hadn't heard from the voice since the day Courtie disappeared. I was about to answer when I realized Becker was watching me intently. Slowly I lowered the receiver into the cradle. "Wrong number," I said.

"Do you get a lot of those?" she asked.

"Our number's almost the same as Chan's." That was true. Chan's is a Chinese restaurant in town that has good take-out food, and our phone number is the same as Chan's except for one digit. We really do get a lot of calls from people wanting to place orders.

I wondered if it was wrong of me not to tell the police about the calls I'd been getting, but I couldn't bring myself to. If Leigh found out, she'd cream me.

It was bad enough that she knew about Courtenay sitting naked at the table. She'd say that if she'd known about the calls, she and Dad would never have left for Saint Bart's. Which was exactly the point. They *needed* that vacation, and I *needed* to prove to Leigh that I was responsible. Besides, the caller only wanted to talk to *me*. The calls didn't have anything to do with Courtie.

Or maybe they did.

Everything was so confusing.

I ran back upstairs to Mike. "Come on. Let's go," I said urgently.

Mike emerged from the bathroom looking fairly presentable. "Okay, I'm ready." He gave his hair a last swipe with his brush.

We walked to the Jacobssens' house, glad to be outdoors for a while. Although the rain had stopped, the night air was still misty and damp. Was Courtenay out in it somewhere? I shivered.

Mike rang the Jacobssens' bell, and Martha let us in. "Hi, you guys," she said, and hugged each of us fiercely, which was not at all like Martha. "Here, let me hang up your coats."

While Martha was getting out coat hangers, Mr. and Mrs. Jacobssen came into the front hall. "Maggie, Mike," said Mrs. Jacobssen warmly. "How are you doing? Courtenay is in our prayers."

I felt embarrassed, since we're not a religious family. I looked at the floor. "Thanks," I said.

Mike managed a smile.

"Come into the living room for a minute before we go downstairs," said Martha.

Mike and I followed her and found ourselves standing before a group of about thirty of Dad and Leigh's friends. They were busily stacking fliers about Courtenay and holding intense conversations in small groups. Five people were clustered around a big map of Princeton and the surrounding towns. It was covered with pushpins indicating where fliers had been handed out and where they were still needed. A few people looked up and greeted us, some with concern, others distractedly, but most just continued working.

"I didn't know your parents were coordinating all this," I said, both surprised and grateful.

Martha nodded proudly. "The police have been a big help, and Mom has even spoken to Search for the Children. They've given us lots of tips, too."

Mrs. Jacobssen was already busy with another couple who had shown up to help, so I just waved to her as Martha and Mike and I went downstairs. Later, I would try to thank Mr. and Mrs. Jacobssen for everything they were doing.

In the Jacobssens' large basement family room, Mike and I found David, Jane, Andrew, and about fifteen other kids. I scanned the crowd quickly and breathed a sigh of relief when I realized that Brad was not there.

"Hey!" exclaimed Mike with a lopsided smile. "What's going on?"

"They're here to help," said Martha.

David stood by me, grinning. "I figured that whatever you wanted to discuss," he said, "had to do with finding your sister. So I decided that the more help you had, the better."

I should have known. David could always be counted on.

"Wow. Thanks everybody." My voice caught, but I managed to keep from crying.

David and Martha and Mike and I joined the other kids on the floor and I got right to the point, doubly determined to find Courtenay since her recovery would also vindicate my mother.

I cleared my throat. "What I wanted to discuss," I said, "are other things we can do to help find Courtenay. The fliers"—I pointed upward to indicate the adults who were working so hard—"are great, but we need posters, too." I held up the poster of Lacey Meigs. "We need to make some of these for Courtenay—as many as we can—and hang them everywhere."

A voice spoke up from the back of the crowd. It was Paul Keane, a friend of Mike's. "My mother owns a printing business. If we do all the work—put the information together, set the type and everything—she'll probably let us make copies for free on cheap cardboard."

"Great! Thanks, Paul," said Mike.

"We could break up into small groups to post them," suggested Jane.

"And if each group gets a car, we could really spread the posters around," added someone else. "We could hit all the towns around here—Lawrenceville, Blawenburg, Skillman, Hopewell, Kingston."

"Fantastic," I said. "And keep in mind that even though we've already been on TV and stuff, we have to make sure we talk to people about Courtenay. Keep her in their thoughts. If you put up a poster in a store, tell the clerk or even the customers about Courtenay. If you're posting them in a neighborhood, tell the residents about her. And be sure to mention the reward." I looked around. Everyone seemed eager to begin.

"Well," said Martha, "let's get started. Pass around the poster, Maggie. Let everyone see it."

And that was how I started my own search for Courtenay.

11

Search for the Children

The next day, Mike and I went back to school. We barely made it to our lockers. Everyone knew about Courtie. Kids who had never spoken to me stopped me in the halls to say they were sorry or, more often than not, to ask what had really happened. They'd been hearing rumors for days. Now they wanted the true, gruesome details.

When I finally reached my locker, I found Martha waiting for me with Paul Keane, whose mother ran the printing business.

"Oh, I'm so glad you're back!" Martha exclaimed as I turned the dial of my combination lock. "I hate it when you're not at school."

"I'm kind of glad to be back myself," I said. "It's awful at home, but now I feel like I'm not doing anything to help."

"Well," said Martha, "the reason Paul and I are

here is because we wanted to suggest that the kids
who are going to help look for Courtenay could eat a
really fast lunch today and then hold a meeting in the
cafeteria about the posters."

"Okay," I said.

"Good," said Martha. "I'll get Mr. Sakala to make
an announcement this morning about the meeting.
Maybe other kids will want to help, too."

More than one hundred students gathered around
Martha and me in the cafeteria at lunchtime that day.
They took over eight of the big tables by the windows. I was astonished. I couldn't believe so many
people cared.

Martha, David, Mike, and I talked to the students
as a panel. We asked them to divide themselves into
groups of three for distributing the posters. There
were thirty-nine groups all together. That meant one
hundred and seventeen kids, counting ourselves.

"Gosh," I said, leaning over to Paul, who was sitting in front of me, "even if we give each group just
fifty posters, which isn't nearly enough, that's almost
two thousand. How many can you really print up? We
ought to give everybody more like a hundred. That's
almost four thousand posters."

Paul gulped. "I hadn't counted on *that* many."

David nudged me. "What's wrong?" he whispered.

I explained.

He slipped his arm around my shoulders, and I
leaned against him gratefully. "I've got an idea," he

said softly, brushing his lips against my ear. David stood up on his chair and cleared his throat. The students, who were trying to divide territory among their groups, fell silent. "Sorry," said David, "but we've just run into a problem. I don't know why we didn't think of this before, but we're going to need some money to run this search. A lot of people will donate their time, materials, and facilities, but not everyone."

A few kids groaned.

David held his hands up. "I'm not asking for donations from you guys," he said, "but we've got to think of some ways to *raise* money—fast."

I spoke up. "Could we organize a bake sale, like by Sunday?" I asked.

"Sure," said a couple of voices.

"The Joggers Club could run a marathon and take pledges for miles run," suggested someone.

"How about a car wash?" said Mike. "We got one together pretty fast to raise money for the earthquake victims last year."

A hand shot up. "I'll be in charge of that."

"Thanks, Nicky," I said. "Listen, everybody, we've only got seven minutes until sixth period. Let me quickly make a list of the things we can do to raise money and then assign people to be in charge of them. Paul, do you think your mom would let you print four thousand posters now, and we could pay her whatever we owe when we've got the money? Kind of an advance?"

"I don't see why not."

"Terrific. Okay, let's assign the projects now." I was really into our meeting. I'd never been much of a leader, but since the cause was *really* important, I found that everything else slipped into unimportance. All that mattered was finding Courtie and clearing my mom. Therefore, all that mattered were posters and bake sales and marathons. I finally felt as if I were really doing something to find my sister.

By the time the meeting was over, six fund-raising projects were under way. Martha, David, Mike, and I were going to be generally in charge—we were to run things, act as troubleshooters, organize the poster distribution, and be the teacher-student liaisons. When the bell rang, I felt as if we'd accomplished a lot.

After school, David and Mike and I went with Paul to his mother's business. Paul had put a sample poster together the night before. Mike and I studied it carefully. MISSING, it said, COURTENAY LOUISE ELLIS. Under the heading was Courtie's photo. And under that were the words *Date Disappeared: April 21, 1986*. Then came Courtie's description, the place where she had last been seen, and even a mention of the suspicious green car. Following the information was the number to call if Courtenay was found or seen.

I stared at the poster and blinked back tears. "It looks fine to me," I managed to say.

"Yeah," Mike added. He turned away from us. In a few short days he'd become somber, completely different from the Mike who used to fool around with the imaginary microphone. ("Okay, Jay, what do we have in the box for Mrs. Tudweiler?")

"All right?" David said, just to make sure.

I nodded.

"I guess we can start printing, then," he told Paul.

So Paul set to work and showed David and Mike and me how to help him. Before we left, which wasn't until six-thirty, I went into Mrs. Keane's office and thanked her profusely.

"I had no idea we'd have to print so *many*," I told her, "but all these kids showed up at the meeting today and they want to help."

Mrs. Keane smiled warmly. "It's the least I can do."

"We'll pay you back whatever you think is fair," I added. "We've figured out lots of ways to raise money, so as soon as we have it—"

Mrs. Keane waved her hand nonchalantly. "Paul and I will work it out later. You concentrate on your sister."

I nodded. "Thanks again." I left her office and found that Paul and Mike were already gone, so David and I walked to my house alone together.

When I got there, I found a woman in our living room talking to Dad, Leigh, and Becker.

Dad stood up as I entered the room. "Hi, sweetie," he said. "How was school?"

"Okay."

There was a pregnant silence. Then Dad tried to make a joke about my cool behavior. "Just okay?" he said, smiling.

"That's right."

Things had been pretty chilly among Leigh, Dad, Mike, and me ever since Dad and Leigh had come home. I was used to the distance between Leigh and me, but not to the one between Dad and me. The situation was not helped by the fact that *I* was creating the distance. Dad, feeling guilty about Mom, was bending over backward trying to set things to rights —and Mike and I wanted nothing to do with him. I didn't think I could ever forgive him. I was even trying to find a way to leave home for the summer—get a job as a camp counselor or something.

My father cleared his throat. "Maggie, I want you to meet someone."

I put my books down on an end table and entered the room. "This is Mrs. Cromwell. She's a friend of Search for the Children. Mrs. Cromwell, this is my daughter, Maggie."

Mrs. Cromwell shook my hand and smiled at me warmly. "I'm called a friend because I'm simply here to help you with anything you need. Search for the Children has friends in many cities and towns across the country. We know this is a difficult time for your family, and we're just here to give a hand. If you need someone to go to the store, to sit by the phone, or just to talk to, give me a call. Any time."

"Thanks," I said.

"I hear you're conducting your own search for your sister."

I nodded. "Over a hundred kids at school are helping." I saw Dad raise his eyebrows. "One boy, Paul Keane, said his mother would donate her printing facilities. We designed a poster, and we're printing four thousand of them." Dad's eyebrows rose higher. "Mrs. Keane can't pay for all four thousand, though, so to raise money we're going to hold a bake sale, a car wash, and stuff like that." I glanced at Leigh to see if she looked impressed, too. I couldn't read her expression, though. "Then the students are going to divide into groups of three with one driver and car per group and distribute the posters as widely as possible. Throughout the county, I guess."

"That's fine," Mrs. Cromwell said approvingly.

The phone rang.

Lamberton leaned out of the kitchen, his eyebrows raised questioningly.

"Would you mind answering it?" Dad asked him.

"Sure thing."

The call was brief. A few seconds later, Lamberton came out of the kitchen. His hands were jammed into his pockets and his face was as gray as a dirty sweatshirt.

Leigh was on her feet immediately. "What is it?" she cried.

Lamberton's eyes flicked from Leigh to Dad to Becker to me and back to Dad, where they settled. "That was Sweeney at the station. Someone found the body of a little girl over in Sussex Woods. It's pretty slashed up, but it matches Courtenay's description. They want someone from your family to go take a look at it."

12

The Body in the Woods

Leigh was hysterical—after she fainted. I'd never seen anybody faint before, not for real. I'd seen ladies swoon in the movies, or TV comedians fall over still as a board in a "dead faint," but I'd never seen a live person faint. Leigh just closed her eyes and went limp all over. Nobody yelled "Catch her!" or anything dramatic like that. Besides, before she fainted she'd sat back down on the couch, so as she slithered over sideways, Dad just took her shoulders and laid her down.

Mrs. Cromwell rose from her chair. "I'll leave now, unless you'd like me to stay."

I shook my head, stunned.

"Here." She handed me a small white card. "This is my phone number. Call me *any* time for *any* reason. I'm here to help."

I thanked her quickly, and she let herself out the front door.

"Maggie, call Dr. Lewis," Dad said.

I didn't hesitate. Leigh was only just coming to and already she sounded hysterical.

Mike walked in the front door as I was hanging up the phone. "Where have you been?" I said accusingly.

"At Andrew's, getting history notes for—"

"Oh, never mind."

Mike took a look around the living room. "What's going on?" he asked.

Before I could answer, Leigh started to scream. "My baby my baby my baby my baby!"

Dad wrapped her tightly in his arms and tried to hold her still.

"What *is* it?" Mike whispered.

I took his elbow and pulled him into the den. "Some cop called Lamberton to say they found the body of a little girl in Sussex Woods."

Mike turned so pale I thought he was going to faint, too.

"Someone has to go look at her. The police say she's all slashed up, but she matches Courtie's description."

"Slashed up?" Mike repeated.

I nodded numbly. I knew what he was thinking. How could somebody "slash up" a four-year-old? When Courtie had first disappeared, I'd tried to convince myself she was just lost. When the police started searching for her body, I'd thought of drowning and other ways of dying accidentally. I had not allowed myself to think of murder. Apparently, Mike hadn't either.

"We better go back," I said to Mike, nodding toward the living room.

Mike looked scared but thoughtful. "Who's going to go look at the body?" he asked.

"Dad, I guess," I answered.

"If he wants someone to go with him, I'll do it."

I put my arm around Mike and we went back to the living room, where Leigh was crying uncontrollably.

"How could they do that?" she screamed. "Why would someone hurt my baby?"

"Honey," Dad said softly, "we don't know that it's Courtie."

"How many four-year-olds are missing in Mercer County?" Leigh demanded.

More than you'd imagine, I thought.

About ten minutes later, Dr. Lewis showed up. He actually made a house call. He and Dad led Leigh upstairs, where Dr. Lewis gave her an injection of something that made her sleepy.

When the men came back downstairs, Dr. Lewis put his hat on and Dad thanked him for coming over as he showed him to the door. Then Dad put his arm around me and said, "Okay, Mike and I are going to go with Detective Lamberton now. I want you to call Leigh's mother and ask her to come over."

"*Dad.*"

Dad had had about as much of me as I had had of him. "Just do it. Leigh needs her mother."

"But—"

"Call her, Maggie."

I really dislike Mrs. Simon. She dyes her hair blue and chain-smokes cigarettes in this long white holder. "I thought she was in Europe," I said.

"She came back this morning, and she knows that Courtenay is missing. She was going to come over here anyway as soon as she recovered from her jet lag." He put his hat on. "Mike and I will be back soon, I hope." Dad, Mike, and Lamberton shrugged into jackets and left the house.

I sighed, sat down in the family room, and reached for the phone. The voice that answered after the fifth ring sounded as if it were speaking around a couple of large jawbreakers. I had to explain three times to Mrs. Simon what had happened. When she finally caught on, she screamed and said she'd be right over.

I hung up the phone. "Swell," I said aloud.

The phone rang again immediately. I was sure it was Mrs. Simon, so I let it ring twice before I picked it up. She probably wanted to know if she could bring us a brisket. Or a roast turkey. She thought we never ate properly unless she fed us.

Finally I picked up the phone. "Hello?"

There was a long pause. "Are you there alone?" whispered the voice.

My stomach lurched.

"No, I'm not," I said shakily.

"Don't lie to me."

"I'm not lying."

"Yes, you are, baby."

Pause.

"How's your sister?" asked the voice.

I jerked my head up. *"What?"*

"Hey, what are you doing right now, baby?" the voice went on smoothly. "I bet you look pretty. I—"

Very slowly, I put my finger on the phone button and depressed it. The line went dead.

And two seconds later, Becker appeared in the doorway, looking stern.

My eyes practically popped out of my head. "I didn't know you were here," I said.

"I just got here. I met your father on his way out. He told me to let myself in. I didn't think you were going to answer the phone. I picked it up in the kitchen."

"You—you heard all that?"

Becker nodded. "Is there something you want to tell me?"

"No."

"Is there something you *ought* to tell me?"

"I guess."

"He asked about Courtenay. How often has that happened?"

"That was the first time!" I cried. "He's never mentioned her before. I swear."

"Just how many of these calls have you gotten, Maggie? And when did they start?"

I sighed. "I don't know how many exactly." I followed Becker into the kitchen and sat down opposite her at the table. "They started about three weeks ago. I've gotten three, maybe four, a week. But he's always just interested in *me*. He's *never* asked about Courtie."

"Why didn't you tell your father or Leigh about the calls?"

"I was embarrassed. The guy asks what I look like, that kind of stuff. I know he means what do I look like naked. I can't tell Dad something like that. And I wouldn't tell Leigh. Besides, he's never said he was coming over or that he knows where I live. I didn't think the calls meant anything—just that some creep dialed our number one day and got a young girl on the phone. Anyway, if I'd said something, Dad and Leigh wouldn't have gone on their honeymoon. And they needed the vacation."

Becker looked very displeased. "Well, why didn't you tell *us* about the calls?"

"Because then you'd have told Dad and Leigh."

Becker put her head in her hands. "Creeps like him can be dangerous," she said. "Do you recognize the voice at all? Does it sound like anyone you know?"

I shook my head. "I can't tell."

"It sounds as if the caller's disguising his voice," Becker remarked. "Maggie, the next time this person calls, please keep him on the line, even if it means leading him on a little. We're going to try to trace his call."

"Okay."

"You realize, don't you, that I'm going to have to

tell your father and stepmother about this? The calls could be critical in finding your sister."

I nodded miserably.

"But," Becker went on, "I'd rather nobody else heard about them. This piece of knowledge will be more useful to us as a secret. If the caller knows we're waiting to trace his calls, he'll stop calling, right?"

"Right. Can I tell Mike about them?"

"I'd just as soon you didn't."

"Why not? He's my brother. He's part of this family and part of the investigation. He won't say anything."

"I'd rather you didn't," Becker repeated.

"Hey, are you accusing Mike of something?" I cried. "Are you saying he's the caller?"

Becker opened her mouth, then closed it.

"Because I've gotten tons of the calls while he was standing right next to me."

"Just keep it to your—" Becker broke off as the front door opened.

My heart skipped a beat.

"Hello-oh!" called a voice.

It was Mrs. Simon. She's asked me about a hundred times to call her Grandma, but I can't bring myself to. "It's Leigh's mother," I whispered to Becker.

I went into the front hall, and there she was, dressed all in white—a white pants suit with a white blouse, white shoes, big white plastic jewelry, a white thing fastened to her hair at the back of her head, and of course the white cigarette holder. The only thing that wasn't white was the cigarette itself, which was pink.

Mrs. Simon embraced me in a cloud of perfume and sympathy. "You poor, poor *dear*," she said. I could tell she was loving every minute of it. Mrs. Simon thrives on drama and emergencies. Her day really improves if, for example, someone dies.

She let go of me and I backed away. "Thanks for coming so...quickly, Mrs. Simon," I said.

"Grandma. Call me Grandma," she corrected me, holding out a foil-wrapped package.

"Oh, gee, thanks. A brisket. How'd you make it so fast?"

"I had it in the freezer. I took it out as *soon* as I returned. It was the very first thing I did. I know your family doesn't eat right. Leigh never did learn how to cook prop—"

Becker had stepped into the room. I introduced her to Leigh's mother, handed her the brisket, and then took Mrs. Simon upstairs, where I left her with Leigh. When I came back into the living room, Becker was sitting on the couch, writing in her notebook. "Quite a woman," she commented.

I made a face. "Did you notice she didn't say a thing about Courtie? All she cares about are her briskets and grand entrances and the excitement."

"Maybe she's just covering up."

"Oh, sure. They find the slashed-up body of a four-year-old thrown in the woods like a piece of garbage, so naturally Mrs. Simon thaws out a brisket and finds a pink cigarette."

Becker attempted a smile, but I burst into tears.

"Maggie," said Becker soothingly.

I tried to stop crying and couldn't. "Can I call Martha?" I said through my tears.

"Of course."

I dialed Martha's number, but it was David who answered the phone. "Maggie?" he said sharply. "What's wrong?"

"Can you come over?"

"I'll be right there."

About ten minutes later, the doorbell rang and David was standing on our front steps, out of breath from running. I opened the door, and he came in and put his arms around me. He held me for a long time before he asked what had happened.

It was funny. Leigh was upstairs being comforted by her mother, and I was downstairs being comforted by David. We should have been comforting each other, but things just never worked out for us. I felt as if I never gained any ground with Leigh. It was always a step forward, a step back, a step forward, a step back. Sometimes two steps back.

"They found a body in the woods, Sussex Woods," I finally told David. "A little girl, all slashed up."

David turned as white as a sheet. "Oh, my God."

"Well, we don't know that it's Courtie," I said as Becker handed me a tissue. I took it gratefully, and David and I sat down on the couch in the living room. Becker ducked out. "Dad and Mike went to... wherever you go, to look at the body. They ought to be back soon, I guess." I wiped my eyes.

David and I sat there holding hands and talking until Dad, Mike, and Lamberton returned. Dad was absolutely ashen. Mike looked green, and in fact went into the bathroom and threw up.

I stood up, and Dad came over to me and put his hands on my shoulders. "It wasn't Courtenay," he said.

"Thank God. What's wrong with Mike?"

"It was a pretty horrible sight."

"Oh."

"Let me go upstairs and talk to Leigh."

"Mrs. Simon's there."

"Good."

"She brought a brisket."

Dad gave me a wry grin and started up the stairs. I grinned back, forgetting momentarily that I was supposed to be mad at him.

I looked at Lamberton. "So who was it?"

"The body?"

"Yeah." Who else? I thought.

"We don't know."

"How can you not know? Hasn't someone reported their daughter missing?"

"Over the last couple of years, thousands. It could be any of them. It could be the child of a runaway who's been missing for years herself. It could be a child who's been missing since birth. It could be a child who *hasn't* been reported missing. Kids, families, fall through the cracks. You'd be surprised."

Mike came out of the bathroom then.

"Are you okay?" David asked him.

Mike nodded. "Yeah. I'm going to try to get some sleep. I'll see you guys tomorrow."

"Good night," we said.

Dad and Mrs. Simon came downstairs a few minutes later, and David took off like a shot. He may be big-hearted, but Mrs. Simon drives even him crazy, which only goes to show how annoying she is.

"Well, 'night, everybody," I said.

Dad looked at his watch. It was only eight-thirty.

I shrugged and ran upstairs. When I reached the top, I slowed down. The door to Dad and Leigh's bedroom was ajar. I peeped in. It was pitch black inside. "Leigh?" I whispered.

No answer.

I pushed the door open. The light from the hall fell across Leigh's face. She was lying on her side, breathing deeply and evenly. She looked peaceful. I tiptoed into the room, sat on the edge of the bed, and put one of her hands between both of mine. She stirred sleepily. "Maggie?" she murmured.

"It's okay, Leigh. Go back to sleep."

"Mmm."

I held her hand for a while longer. Then I placed it gently on the blanket and tiptoed back out, closing the door behind me.

13

The Search Continues

The next five days became a blur of school, police-men, and meetings and fund-raising projects with our friends and the kids at school. We held our first bake sale, hastily arranged, and it was such a success that we decided to hold another the following weekend. Mike and I tried desperately to catch up on our missed schoolwork and to keep up with the new work, but it was impossible. I decided to resign my-self to summer school. Just then, Courtie seemed more important than classes.

On Tuesday evening, I was sitting alone in the den, working on Courtenay projects. Dad was in the kitchen talking to Lamberton (Becker wasn't around much anymore), and Mike was over at Paul Keane's house, helping him stack the posters into packs of fifty. I was scribbling away so furiously that I didn'⁺

hear Leigh. I wasn't even aware that she had come into the den until she sat down beside me.

I jumped and dropped my pen. "You scared me!"

"I'm sorry, honey. I didn't mean to. You were writing so busily."

I looked at Leigh. She was wearing the same robe she'd had on for days—ever since the TV news interview. There were huge dark rings under her eyes, and because she'd been living mainly on coffee since she and Dad got back from Saint Bart's, she was visibly thinner, especially around her cheekbones.

That was the first time she'd spoken to me voluntarily since the day they returned.

"What are you working on?" she asked tiredly, rubbing her forehead.

I paused. "Courtenay stuff..."

"Courtenay stuff?"

"For our search. We printed up four thousand posters about Courtie. Then, to pay for them, we held a bake sale, which earned almost two hundred and fifty dollars, a car wash, which earned about the same amount, and a jogging marathon, which earned three hundred dollars. We've already paid for the posters, we have money left over, and we still have a bunch of other projects to do. All the money's going into a Search for Courtenay Fund. Mr. Sakala at school helped us set it up." I couldn't look at Leigh. I was afraid of what I'd see.

"Who's 'us'?" was all she said.

"Me, Mike, David, Martha, Jane, Andrew, and a

hundred and forty-one kids at school. More join us every day."

Leigh nodded. "Maggie, why didn't you come to your father and me when you started getting the obscene phone calls?"

I'd been waiting for that question. "Because I was embarrassed," I replied. "And because I was afraid you'd give up your vacation if you knew about them."

"But don't you think it would have been wiser for us to stay home?"

"I don't know. I didn't want to be the cause of that."

"What do you mean, Maggie?"

"Everything's always my fault around here!" I blurted out. "I mess up with Courtenay, I cause problems with you and Mike and me, I make dumb mistakes, I'm not reliable. The last thing I wanted was to be responsible for ruining your vacation." My eyes filled with tears.

Leigh reached out and took my hand. "Honey, I'm sorry," she said.

"Me, too," I sniffed.

"I'm impressed with all the money you've earned," she said. "Very impressed."

"Thanks.... You want to help us?"

"I don't think so."

"But Leigh, it's for Courtie."

Silence. Then, "You're doing a good job with the search," she said finally, and left the room.

I sat there bristling. It wasn't that Leigh didn't want to help find Courtie. She just didn't want to help *me* do it.

I was glad the fund-raising projects were going so well, but what concerned me the most were the posters. They would be the most helpful in locating Courtenay. As fast as Mike and Paul could sort the posters into stacks, kids came and got them and put them up. They were all over the county. You couldn't go more than two steps without seeing Courtie's giggly face smiling at you from a lamppost or phone pole, or from inside a store window.

On Wednesday afternoon, the day after my talk with Leigh, David and I decided to put up a stack of posters as well as some of the Jacobssens' fliers. "Let's take Hopewell instead of Cranberry," I said as I climbed into his car. "I know we haven't hit Cranberry yet, but Hopewell isn't too far from here, so we should cover it soon."

"Okay, boss," replied David. He slid behind the wheel, and we took off for Hopewell.

"Look how green everything is, David," I said after we'd been driving for a while. "You know, I've been so wrapped up in Courtenay, I've been forgetting other things, important things—like the fact that summer's on the way."

"You know what else is on the way?"

"What?"

"The Junior Prom."

I froze. Then a pleasant, tingly feeling began to creep up my body, starting in my toes. "The Prom?" I repeated breathlessly.

"Yeah.... Would you like to go?"

I couldn't believe it! Would I like to go? Would I

like a million dollars? Would I like to have Courtie back? Of course I wanted to go! I'd been dreaming of going to a prom ever since I first heard of them. I was wild to go. But I simply said demurely, "Oh, David. Thank you! I'd love to."

"Great," he said. He reached over and squeezed my hand, then returned to his driving. David is a serious, careful driver.

I leaned back and closed my eyes for a few moments. I wanted a white gown. White couldn't possibly clash with red hair. Something simple would be nice—maybe spaghetti straps and a full skirt.

Suddenly I jerked upright. What was I doing? How did I dare daydream about something as lovely as my first prom when Courtie was *missing?*

"It's such a mystery," I said.

"What is?" asked David.

"Courtie. She gets on the school bus, but she never gets *to* school, and nobody notices when she disappears. She couldn't just vanish into thin air."

"No," said David.

"But do you know how many weird cases of missing people there are? I mean, famous cases. Like Judge Crater. In 1930, he stepped into a cab in New York City—and was *never heard from again.* Not a single trace of him was found. If he was murdered, his body should have been found. If he was still alive, somebody should have seen him. Then there was Dorothy Arnold. In 1910—I think it was 1910— she said goodbye to a friend she'd been chatting with

in front of a store in New York, crossed Fifth Avenue
—and was never heard from again. Or that famous
writer Ambrose Bierce. He investigated one of the
strangest cases of disappearance ever—this guy
Orion Williamson really *did* vanish into thin air, right
in front of the eyes of his family—and then Bierce
himself disappeared. It was about sixty years later.
He left the United States, crossed into Mexico—and
was never heard from again."

"Those stories are *bizarre*," said David. "Are you
sure they're true?"

"Well, that's how they've been documented, by lots
of different writers and journalists. I get goose bumps
just thinking about them. And there are plenty more
stories like them. I'd die to know what happened to
those people, but I guess we'll never find out."

"Yeah." David slowed down, stopped at a light, and
turned left onto the road that would take us to Hopewell. "But you know, I bet it wouldn't be so hard to
disappear if you really wanted to. I mean right now, if
we just kept on driving, we could probably disappear
so that no one would ever hear from us again. Nobody
knows where we're headed. Back at Paul's, we said
we were going to cover Cranberry, and then we
changed our minds as we got in the car. If we drove
another hundred miles or so, we could take this car to
a junkyard to be crushed by a compactor, then buy
bus tickets to some little town in the middle of nowhere, change our identities.... I bet we could do
it."

"David!" I said with a gasp. "*That* is bizarre."

"Bizarre, but possible."

"I suppose so. Why would anyone want to do that, though?"

David shrugged. "Who knows? An impossible marriage, escaping from trouble or the law. It's better than killing yourself or something."

I shivered. "But Courtie's only four. Those things don't apply to her."

"No, that's true. I'm just pointing out that every mystery does have a solution, even if we don't know what it is, and some of those solutions are probably pretty mundane. But the mysteries remain mysteries because we don't know what the solutions are. Judge Crater could simply have gotten fed up with his life and taken off for a cabin in the mountains or something. His story just seems more frightening because we don't know what really happened."

"You're too practical!" I teased. "Those mysteries fascinate me."

"You're too romantic," David teased back, smiling. "But don't change. I like you that way."

We were driving slowly along the main street of Hopewell. When David found a parking space, he maneuvered the car into it and we got out, armed with posters and fliers.

"Well?" said David.

"I guess we might as well split up and each take one side of the street."

"Yeah. I was thinking the same thing, even though

it would be more fun to do this together." Hopewell
is such a quaint little town that people come every
day just to look around and window-shop and buy
gifts. Consequently, a lot of stores have sprung up recently and the town is a busier place than it used to
be. We'd get a lot more accomplished separately than
together.

For the next hour, I pounded the pavement. I
tacked posters to phone poles, lampposts, signposts,
fences, and mailboxes. I went into every store, asked
the clerks for permission to put a poster in the window, and made a point of telling them about Courtie
and her disappearance. I walked up to strangers on
the street, handed them fliers, and said, "This is my
sister. She's missing. Have you seen her?"

Most people looked at me as if I were crazy and
walked on, not even taking a flier. But some stopped,
asked questions, and chatted. A lot of the ones who
stopped were parents and grandparents with little
kids in tow. Obviously they were worried about their
own children. "Please keep your eyes open," I said.
"Eventually Courtenay will have to be taken to a doctor or walked through some public place or enrolled
in school. She's almost five."

"I surely will," said one older woman. "And I'll put
your sister in my prayers."

"Thanks," I said.

It was when I returned to David's car to get more
fliers that I first noticed the battered green station
wagon. It was double-parked next to David's car, the

motor running, a driver at the wheel.

The second time I noticed it was about twenty minutes later. I'd been working my way along the street when I turned around suddenly to pick up a handkerchief that a man had dropped when I'd handed him a flier. The car was behind me. Was it following me? The figure at the wheel ducked his (her?) head so that I couldn't see the face.

My palms began to sweat. I walked into a store. When I came out, the green car was still there. I ran for a block and glanced over my shoulder. The car was right behind me. I headed for a side street, then turned suddenly and dashed across the main street in front of the station wagon. I was going against the light, so the car had to brake suddenly. And as it did, I turned and faced the driver head-on. It was a woman, but that was all I could tell. She was wearing sunglasses, and the sun was reflected in the windshield. The woman stepped on the gas as soon as I was out of her path and zoomed through the intersection—but not before I noted the license plate. I committed it to memory for Lamberton and ran in search of David.

14

Going Nowhere Fast

"David!" I called. I reached the other side of the street and tried to find David and keep an eye on the green car at the same time. But the car was soon out of sight. As I watched, it screeched to a halt at a red light, then turned and sped out of Hopewell.

I looked up and down the street. "David!" I called again.

At that moment he emerged from a coffee shop.

"Hey!" he greeted me cheerfully. "I just ran out of posters. How are you doing?"

"We have to get to the police! We have to find a phone!" I cried. "I was being followed. By a—a green car. It's a clue to Courtenay. I know it. I got the license plate. I mean, I think I did. It's C-N-O, six-six-one. Or was it six-one-one? No, it was definitely six-six-one. David, come *on!*"

"Wait! Maggie! What are you talking about? A green car?"

"It was following me. There was a lady inside."

"Are you sure it was following you?"

"Positive."

"You think it has something to do with Courtenay? Couldn't it just have been some kook? Maybe it was a guy. You know, some creepo who wanted you to get in the car with him or something."

"No, no! It was a woman. And Lamberton said that on the morning Courtie disappeared, someone spotted an old green Ford on the street outside her school. I've got to call Lamberton and see if the license plates match."

David's eyes opened wide. "Maggie," he said slowly. "Does this mean you're in danger, too? Is this person after you now?"

"Oh, my God! I don't know. I was just thinking about how this would help us find Courtie."

"Come on. We've got to get you home before anything happens."

"No, I want to call Lamberton first! I want him to check the license plate right away."

David looked frantic. He looked as if he were literally being pulled in two different directions. "Okay, okay," he said. "There's a phone booth. Let's go. I want to do this fast."

I'd never seen David so scared, which only made me more scared. He hustled me up the block, across a side street, and into the booth. Then he shoved the door closed and stood in front of it, trying to watch the sidewalk and the street at the same time.

My fingers shook as I dropped a coin in the slot. I waited impatiently for someone to answer the phone.

"Hello?" It was Leigh. Her expectant voice made me flinch guiltily.

"Leigh, it's me, Maggie. Is Lamberton there, please? I've got to talk to him."

"Honey, where are you? Is something wrong? Are you okay?"

"Oh, Leigh." Suddenly I almost wished she were there with me. "I saw a green car. It was following me. I was so scared. And someone saw a green Ford the day Courtie disappeared. Please. I have the license number for Lamberton."

"Okay, sweetheart," said Leigh calmly. "It's all right. Here he is."

But when Lamberton got on the phone, he said the last thing I wanted to hear. "The person who spotted the car gave us a very general description and didn't get the license plate. If he had, we would already have traced it or tried to trace it."

"Didn't get it?" I couldn't hide the disappointment in my voice.

"No, but that's all right. We'll check into the number you noted and see what's what. Very likely it's nothing at all."

"This car was old and beat up," I persisted. "Is that what the other person said?"

"Yes."

"And it was a Ford station wagon?"

"Yes."

"It has to be the same car! Do you think they're after me?"

"It's unlikely, Maggie, but why don't you come on home now. Is anyone with you?"

"Yes, David."

"Good. Try to calm down. We'll see you in about twenty minutes, okay?"

"Okay." I hung up. "David, let's go. Lamberton wants me home."

"Right."

We tore back to the car and jumped in. I'm not sure why we were so afraid, since the green car was out of sight. I think it was just that any little incident could make all our fears come pouring forth. It's amazing how vulnerable we can feel.

"Lock the doors," David said urgently.

I did so, and he floored the car. I mean *floored* it. We roared out of Hopewell at a speed that probably hadn't ever been recorded there.

"Watch out the back. Make sure we're not being followed. I can't watch and drive at the same time," said David.

I watched, but I didn't see anything suspicious. Even so, neither of us began to breathe easier until we turned into my driveway.

I ran inside with David close behind me and, much to my surprise, ran right into Leigh's arms. If Dad had been there, I might have run to him, despite all our bad feelings, but he wasn't home.

"Leigh, that was so scary!" I cried. "What if they're after *me*?"

Leigh didn't say a word. She just held me and patted my back.

After several seconds I heard Lamberton say gently, "It won't hurt you to be extra careful from now on, Maggie. Mike, too. I know this is a touchy subject with you, but if your mother is involved, it would make sense that she'd want to take you and Mike. You're the ones she's really after."

"That—that *person* in that *car* was not my mother," I said through clenched teeth.

"Maybe not," replied Lamberton, "but she could have hired someone to abduct you. That's not uncommon."

"My mother wouldn't do that!"

"Honey, calm down," Leigh said soothingly. I was still clinging to her.

I sighed and smiled at her shakily. Then I turned to Lamberton. Before I could utter another word, he said, "We already ran that license plate through our computers."

"You did?" I forgot to be angry with him.

"It belongs to a car that's leased through a rental agency."

"Someone *paid* to drive around in that wreck?" I exclaimed.

Leigh and Lamberton smiled. "It was a *cheap* car rental agency," Lamberton explained. "Very cheap. At any rate, the car was rented about two weeks ago to a Miss Jean Farmer of Lawrenceville. We checked the street address she gave. It doesn't exist. And apparently she paid with cash, so there are no credit cards to check. There's no way to trace her. Fake name, probably, and fake address."

"Are they sure it was a woman?" I asked. "Jean can be a man's name."

"Probably not spelled that way, though," said Lamberton. "And I'll admit that the car rental agency is a bit of a dump, but someone there would have noticed if a man filled out the forms using a woman's name."

I glanced at Leigh. "It's just that I was thinking that Jack...Mr. Tierno...well, he lives in Lawrenceville and..."

"True enough," said Lamberton, "but he has an airtight alibi."

Leigh let out the breath she'd been holding. We were both glad Jack wasn't in trouble, but my mother wasn't off the hook yet. All our clues seemed to be leading us nowhere fast.

I turned to David.

"I better go," he said. (I was about to ask him to stay.) "I don't want to be in the way."

Leigh looked sort of relieved to hear this, so I decided not to push anything. All the excitement must have been making her nervous. And she was just beginning to get better. She was even dressed that day, and had eaten breakfast.

"Okay," I said to David. "Listen, would you mind tracking Mike down on your way home? He's probably still at Paul's, but he might be over at Andrew's. He should come home so we can tell him about the car and warn him to be careful."

"No problem."

I walked David to the front door. He kissed me quickly, then pulled me to him and held me close for a long time. "Please be careful," he whispered as we drew apart.

"I will."

David turned and at that moment the front door burst open.

I screamed.

Lamberton and Leigh came running.

"What is it?"

"Hi! I'm h—" Mike started to say as he bolted inside. Andrew was behind him. They stopped short. "What's wrong?"

David, Leigh, Lamberton, and I all went limp, as if we were deflating balloons. "Nothing," I answered. "We're just a little jumpy. Listen, Mike, Detective Lamberton and I have to talk to you. Something happened this afternoon."

"Courtie?" he asked quickly.

I shook my head. "No. No news, but we have to talk."

David stepped out the door. "Come on, Andrew. We'll see you guys tomorrow."

The boys left, and Mike followed me into the living room to hear about Miss Jean Farmer and the green car.

15

Caught!

Ring, ring.

It was three o'clock on the Saturday after the green car episode. Lamberton had just shown up and was talking to Dad, Leigh, Mike, and me in the living room. He had no real news, though.

The phone interrupted us. "I'll get it," I said, standing up. *Don't let it be Mrs. Simon,* I prayed as I dashed into the kitchen. *And please let it be David.*

"Hello?" I said.

There was a pause. "Hi, baby. Are you there alone?"

I froze. Then I waved frantically at Lamberton, who figured out what was going on and gestured to me to calm down and to keep talking. He dashed up to Leigh's studio to make a call on her private line.

I fingered the little device that was still attached to the phone, and tried to think of something to say to

126

the caller. "I'm—I'm—" Would he want me to be alone or not? I took a chance. "Yes, I am alone...are you?"

"I'm always alone, baby. Why don't we get together?"

"I...don't have a car. What do you mean you're always alone? Don't you have any"—asking if he didn't have any friends was sort of pathetic, and I didn't want to make him mad—"a family? Or a job to go to?"

"It doesn't matter, baby. No one understands me. That's why I'm always alone—in my head, you know?...So what are you wearing?"

"Well, I'm wearing my jeans and a sweat shirt—"

"The yellow-and-white one?"

The yellow-and-white one? I *was* wearing my yellow-and-white sweat shirt. Could the caller *see* me? And if not, how did he know I had a yellow-and-white sweat shirt in the first place? My heart skipped several beats. Little drops of cold sweat formed on my upper lip.

I tried to keep my voice from shaking, as I replied, "Yes, it's the yellow-and-white one. And I have gold hoops in my ears, and barrettes in my hair."

"Very nice."

Mike, Dad, and Leigh were all watching me tensely.

The voice spoke again. "If you're alone, baby, I could come over to your house."

My mind was jumping around as if it were wired.

"If you come over," I finally said, "what, um, what do you want to do? We have a VCR—"

"I know you do, baby." *He knows?* "I just want to be with you, that's all. What do you need that boyfriend for, anyway?"

"Who, David?"

"Yeah, him."

I swallowed hard. My fingers were gripping the phone so tightly that my knuckles had turned white. I laughed nervously. "Oh, he's just a good friend, you know? We just hang around together."

"Well, I don't like it. You stay away from him."

"Sure. Whatever you say." I giggled.

"It's nothing to laugh at, baby."

"No. No, of course not," I said quickly. At that moment, Lamberton returned to the kitchen, making a slashing motion at his throat to indicate that I could hang up.

"Listen," I told the caller, "I have to go. We'll get together soon, I promise." I hung up and sank into a chair.

Lamberton looked grim, but he said, "Beautiful, Maggie. You did that perfectly...just right. We got it all—phone number, address. The caller doesn't live too far away."

"I'm not surprised," I managed to say. "He knows me."

"What do you mean?" cried Leigh.

"He knows we have a VCR. He knows I have this yellow-and-white sweat shirt. He even guessed that I

was wearing it. ... I thought maybe he could see me,"
I said with a sob. "Oh, God. I'm so scared. There are
people following me and people threatening me over
the phone. They took my little sister. Why are they
after me? No one's safe anymore. No one's safe."

With a single movement, Dad and Leigh came toward me, enfolding me in their arms. "I tried to protect Courtie," I cried. "I tried to. And it didn't work. I
can't even protect myself. It's so unfair. If someone's
after you, they can get you, as long as they're on the
offensive and you're on the defensive. They just need
a little violence or some threats and that's it."

"It makes you feel violated, doesn't it?" Leigh murmured in my ear.

"I guess so. It's like they have some power over
you. They can see you and they can reach right into
your life and scare you or hurt you or...worse."

I sensed that the discussion wasn't nearly over, but
Lamberton cleared his throat and announced, "The
call was coming from five-five-five-two-one-eight-
three at Forty-six Rosedale Road. That's not too far
away, is it?"

Mike, who by then was rummaging around in the
refrigerator, dropped the platter holding the remains
of Mrs. Simon's brisket.

And I shrieked.

"What—" Lamberton started to ask.

"That's the de Christophers' number." Mike's face
was ashen. "Andrew?" he croaked.

I shook my head. "Brad. The caller must be Brad."

I was right. The police went over to the de Christophers' house that afternoon and arrested him. He was the only one home. I was glad of that, because it meant there was no chance of Andrew being a suspect. Brad was clearly the guilty party. Also, Jane and Andrew didn't have to see their brother being arrested. Small blessings, I guess.

Brad was taken to the police station, questioned, charged with harassment, and released on bail. The biggest mistake he had made in his phone calls was asking about Courtie, even if he had done it only once. It didn't look great that he'd been hanging around our house the afternoon of the television interview, either, but that was explained away later. The important thing was that Brad had not taken Courtie. He had nothing to do with her. I was almost sorry. I wanted the kidnapper to be Brad, just to prove that my mother wasn't guilty.

"Brad used the oldest trick in the book," Lamberton told us later as we gathered in the living room to hear his news.

"The oldest trick?" I repeated.

"He put a handkerchief over the phone when he spoke to you. Otherwise you'd have recognized his voice."

"But why? Why was he harassing me?"

"He said he wanted you to be his girlfriend." I shuddered. "He said he's always liked you, and that when you started going out with David, he felt he had to do something to get your attention."

"Well, why didn't he just call and say, 'Hi. Maggie, this is Brad. Would you like to go out with me sometime?' I'd never have gone out with him, but that seems to me to be the normal way to approach things."

"Maggie," Mike spoke up, "you know he's not normal."

I saw my father look at Mike sharply.

"Well, he's not," said Mike, "and I'm glad somebody finally got to him. He's had the rest of us trapped for years."

"What do you mean?" asked Leigh. "He's so much older than you. I didn't know you saw him that often."

Mike explained. I joined in. All the years of torturing and threatening and blackmail came pouring out. Dad and Leigh shook their heads.

"What was he doing watching our house last week?" I asked Lamberton. "Was he curious about Courtie?"

"Not really. He used the curiosity-seekers as an excuse to watch for *you*. He just wanted to see you, to see what you were doing."

"I wish he'd had to stay in jail. I'm afraid of him."

"I'm sorry," said Lamberton. "His bail's been paid. There's no reason to keep him in jail."

I burst into tears. "Dad, I'm sorry I got mad at you," I said. "I still don't think Mom is guilty and I still don't think you were right to make decisions about Mike and me and our custody behind our backs, but we can't be angry. We need each other too much right now."

"Come here, Maggie." I crossed the room and sat next to my father on the couch, laying my head against his shoulder.

"Dad?" asked Mike.

"It's okay, son. You don't have to say anything."

Lamberton left the room and the rest of us sat together in needy silence.

16

The Return of Jessica Ellis

If anyone were to ask me to look back on the spring that Courtie disappeared and associate one word with it, I would have to say *telephone*. It seemed that any important or scary happening was signaled by the phone. Even before Dad and Leigh left for their vacation, the phone was ringing with Brad's anonymous calls. It rang with Leigh's unfortunate call from Saint Bart's. Later, it rang with news of Courtie. It rang when the body was found in the woods. And one day, it rang with a call from a run-down diner in upstate New Jersey.

The caller was Jessica Ellis, my mother.

By then, Courtie had been missing for nineteen days, and the detectives were running out of clues to follow up. The FBI had been unable to trace my mother. Mr. Tierno was not a suspect. Birdie was no longer a suspect. And nothing could be done about

Miss Jean Farmer and the rented car until she returned it, at which time the rental agency was to call the police. There wasn't much you could do with a fake name and address. The state police were to watch for the car, though.

Brad had been caught, and no ransom calls were coming in. Even Lamberton himself wasn't around much by then, although he stopped by about once a day to see what was going on. Dad had started going into the office part-time. Life was returning to normal. Except that we didn't have Courtenay. I began to wonder if she was dead after all.

And then the phone rang.

It rang at ten o'clock on a Saturday morning. I was sitting in the kitchen looking forlornly at a math paper. It was a review sheet for my geometry final, and not a thing on it made sense. Mike was sitting across the table from me, annoyed because he was supposed to be tutoring me, and nothing he did or said seemed to help me understand the problems better. I had simply missed too many classes that spring, and anyway, it was hard to concentrate.

Leigh was in her studio on the second floor. I knew that illustrations for a picture book were due to a publisher two weeks from then. I also knew that she'd barely worked on them since about a week before she and my father had left for Saint Bart's. Furthermore, I knew that although she was panicked about getting the assignment done on time, she just wasn't able to work on it for any extended period of time.

Dad was upstairs, too. He'd been on the phone all morning, contacting various service organizations, lawyers, and private detectives. The police may have been slowing down their involvement with us, but Dad couldn't stop searching. I wasn't sure whether he was looking for my mother or for Courtenay.

When the phone rang, I assumed it was for Dad, but I made a grab for it anyway, hoping David might have been trying to get through. Besides, I couldn't look at one more theorem or corollary.

"Hello?" I said.

There was a pause. Then a woman's voice asked simply, "Maggie?"

Here's how wrapped up I was in my geometry: I actually thought the caller was Mrs. Taylor, my teacher, calling at home to check up on me.

I glanced guiltily at Mike. "Yes?" I said.

"Maggie Ellis?"

"Yes?...Mrs. Taylor?"

"No. Maggie, this is your mother."

"What?" I whispered.

"It's Mommy, sweetheart."

I didn't seem able to raise my voice. "Where are you?" I whispered.

Mike looked up from my math paper and raised his eyebrows, asking a silent question. I wanted to cup my hand over the mouthpiece of the phone and tell him who was calling, but I couldn't move.

"Not too far away, darling. I'm in Ridgewood, New Jersey. I want to see you."

We had done an excellent job of keeping Mom's name out of the news, out of the story altogether. As we had promised Lamberton, we hadn't mentioned that angle of the case to a soul. At least I hadn't, and I assumed the others hadn't either. Because if Mom had gotten wind of it, she'd never have dared to get so close to Princeton.

"You want to see us?" I repeated. Why couldn't I say anything intelligent?

By that time, Mike had gotten to his feet and was standing behind me. "What's going on, Maggie? Is it about Courtenay?"

I shook my head. "No. It's Mom. It's our *mother*. She wants to see us."

"Where is she?" Mike clenched his jaw, and I could see a muscle under his ear working up and down, up and down.

"Maggie? Are you still there?" asked Mom. "I know this is a surprise, but—"

I waved Mike away. "Yes. Yes, I'm here. You're in Ridgewood, Mom? When do you want to see us?"

"Today. Can you get away? It's Saturday."

I didn't answer her question. "How come you never tried to see us before?"

"I wasn't permitted to."

"But you aren't now, either, are you? Why—"

"Not so many questions, darling. Let me give you directions to Ridgewood. Mike can drive, can't he?"

"Yes." All I could think of was how warm I felt, talking on the phone to my own mother, hearing her call me "darling." That word didn't have the same meaning coming from the lips of anyone else, not even my father. The bond between mother and daughter is unique, and very strong. It can stand a lot. It would have to, I thought, in order for a simple word to turn my knees to oatmeal, and to make me forget everything Dad had told Lamberton about Jessica Ellis.

"Do you have paper and pencil?"

"Um, yes.... Just a sec." I scrambled around for a pen and a pad of notepaper. "Okay."

Mom gave me directions to a motel and diner on the outskirts of Ridgewood. "Bring a map of New Jersey with you just in case. And Maggie?"

"Yeah?"

"Don't tell anyone where you're going. Not the police and not your father."

"All right."

"You're a good girl. I'll be waiting, sweetheart."

In slow motion, I returned the receiver to the cradle. "Mike," I said in a low voice, "she wants to see us to*day*. She's in Ridgewood at some diner or motel. She gave me directions. I know we shouldn't go, and I know we should tell Lamberton, but if Dad keeps up this custody thing, we might not have another chance to see her for years. I think we should go ahead. We can see for ourselves that Mom doesn't have Courtie. Then we'll come home, tell everyone all about it, and Mom's name will be clear and she'll be off somewhere before anyone can do anything to her. What do you think?"

A slow grin spread across Mike's face. His hand

gripped an imaginary microphone, and in his best announcer's voice, he said, "Folks, it's truly inspiring. These people, separated for so many years, are about to be reunited by the miracle of the telephone and a VW Rabbit—and you are here to witness the emotional and blessed event."

I grabbed Mike, kissed his cheek, and cried, as loudly as I dared, "I can't be*lieve* it! We're going to get to see her! I wonder how she'll look. Remember her hair—all kind of scraggly and wild, like she—"

"Not now, Maggie. In the car. We've got to get going." Mike ran to the base of the stairs and yelled up, "Hey, Dad! Leigh! David and Martha want to go to the beach! We're taking the car! We're going to..."

"Asbury Park," I whispered.

"Asbury Park! Okay? We'll be back by seven. See you."

Mike and I grabbed a couple of apples and some beach towels to make our trip look legitimate, but we didn't even bother with our suits since we'd have had to go upstairs for them. On our way to the garage, I could hear Leigh calling out something about my geometry exam, but I didn't answer her. We jumped into the car, and Mike sped down the driveway and headed for Route 1.

"How long do you think it will take to get there?" I asked.

"About an hour, I guess. Maybe an hour and a half. Depends on the roads."

"Oh, Mike, *finally*. After all this time we're going to

see her. Mom. I knew she'd call us one day."

"Remember the time it was snowing and she arranged an indoor picnic supper on the floor in the living room?"

"And let us roast hotdogs in the fireplace?" I added. "And remember the time she and Dad had company for dinner and Mom was carrying the chicken into the dining room and dropped the whole platter on the floor, and just said, as calmly as ever, 'I'm *so* sorry, I'll go get the other one'—but of course there was no other one; Mom just put the dropped one back on the platter."

Mike laughed. "Do you remember the time we were bored and she told us we could paint the tile walls in the bathroom with watercolors?"

"Yeah. And when I was little and you were at school and Dad was at work, did you know that Mom would sit on the floor in my room and play dolls with me? Not many mothers would do that.... Mike?"

"What."

"Do you remember any of the stuff Dad told Lamberton about?"

Mike hesitated. "I don't think so."

"I don't think so, either."

Mike pressed the blinker down and turned left onto Route 1.

We lapsed into silence.

17

Mom

The directions Mom had given me led us to a stark, seedy highway just south of Ridgewood. We could see nothing but sleaze, as Mike put it, in all directions. We passed run-down gas stations, the price signs swinging back and forth in the breeze. We passed squat motels, paint peeling, the numbers on the room doors fading. They had funny names like Sleep-E-Hollow and Bed 'n' Bite and E-Z Nite. One even advertised rooms for rent.

"Can you imagine living in one of those awful motel rooms right on the highway?" I asked Mike.

He set his jaw. "You'd have to be pretty desperate," he replied.

We passed diners, blinds drawn against the sun, broken glass scattered through the parking lots. Some of them looked abandoned. A blackboard was set out in front of one. In childish handwriting, it advertised:

Today's Special—Cheese Sandwich— 50¢.

"That's a special?" I said.

"Could you look at the directions again?" asked Mike. "Either we've passed the turnoff or we're right on top of it. Mom said two and a half miles on this road, and we passed that almost half a mile ago."

"We're watching for the American Tile Company," I told Mike, "or a sign that says American Tile Company. I'm not sure whi— Hey, there it is." Looming up on our right was a billboard, the paper peeling away at the edges. A fat cartoon workman wearing a white cap and overalls was holding up a piece of tile twice his size. AMERICAN TILE CO., the sign screamed. TILE FOR ALL YOUR NEEDS. "Okay, turn right," I instructed. "Yeah, this is the road. Now we're looking for Annie's."

"Annie's?"

"That's what Mom said. It's a motel with a diner. She said there'd be a big sign and the diner is trimmed in red. It should be on the right."

We passed an old gas station, no longer in use, and a low, flat-roofed brick building that could have been anything—once. The broken windows were boarded up and trash was blowing through the parking lot. A newspaper had flattened itself against the front door.

"Mike?" I said. "I don't like this place."

"What place?"

"Here. This area. There's something almost obscene about it. There aren't even any people around."

Mike didn't answer me. He was gazing intently

down the road, shading his eyes with one hand. "There's Annie's," he said.

We pulled into a parking lot that was just as full of trash and broken glass as any other we'd passed. There were, however, three cars parked in the lot, all of which looked as if they were on their last legs—or last wheels. The lot stretched around behind the diner, a wasteland of pavement.

"Park in front," I said nervously. "I don't want to get too far from the road."

Mike obliged. We eased ourselves out of the Rabbit, emerging at the same time. Our eyes met over the top of the car.

"Lock it," said Mike.

I ducked down, locked the door, then stood again. "I *really* don't like this place," I said nervously. "It's creepy. I feel as if we've wandered into the Twilight Zone or something."

Mike was grappling with some problem. "Look," he said after a moment, peering at the dirty windows of Annie's Diner, "maybe you should leave your door unlocked, just in case. That way we can get in fast if we have to." He tossed me the keys and I unlocked my door. Then I ran around to Mike and grasped his arm. We approached the diner.

Annie's Diner looked as if once it might actually have been a dining car on a train. It was made of metal, long ago gone grimy, and was shaped like a train car. But attached to one end was a ramshackle building with a sign identifying it as the OFICE, and attached to the other end was a long structure with a row of doors numbered 1 through 6. Annie's Motel.

"You don't think Mom's *staying* here, do you?" I asked Mike, shuddering.

He shrugged, frowning.

We climbed the steps to the diner, and Mike opened the door for me. When my eyes adjusted to the dim light inside, I was surprised. The diner didn't look so bad after all. At any rate, it was clean, which was more than I had expected. The heavy smell of coffee that greeted us was very reassuring.

A thin older woman (Annie?) who reminded me of Birdie was standing behind the counter, a pot of coffee in her hand.

"Can I help you kids?" she asked pleasantly.

I looked around. There were six booths in the diner and ten counter stools. The booths were empty, but two of the stools at one end of the counter were occupied by old men. A third stool, at the opposite end, was taken by a teenage boy.

"We're—we're waiting for someone," I said.

"Well, have a seat. Anywhere." The woman waved her hand vaguely in front of her.

Mike and I sat down in one of the booths.

The woman approached us immediately, armed with the coffeepot. I saw that a name tag was pinned to her white uniform. *My name is Verna,* it said. *I'm here to serve you."*

"Coffee?" asked Verna.

"Yes, please."

Verna turned over two of the cups that were waiting face down on the table. She filled them and left.

"Where is she?" I whispered to Mike. "Where's Mom? I thought she was already here. I mean, I thought she was calling from here. Look, there's a pay phone by the door.... I thought she'd be here," I said again.

Mike stirred his coffee idly, even though he hadn't put cream or sugar in it. "This isn't the place I'd imagined for a reunion of long-lost relatives," he said.

I rubbed my eyes tiredly. "You don't suppose she's —could she have... it would be kind of like her not to show up after all. I mean, it would be like our laid-back Mom, not like Dad's desperate Jessica. Maybe we're just too much responsibility."

"I think she'll show up," said Mike without conviction.

"Really?"

"I don't know. I don't think she would have risked getting in touch with us and have asked us to drive all the way up here if she didn't really want to see us. She's never tried something like this. And she had it pretty well planned, giving us those specific directions and all. Besides, we didn't arrange a time to meet."

"That's true. How long do you think we should wait?"

"An hour," said Mike firmly. "An hour is long enough."

I was sitting on the side of the booth that faced the

front door of the diner, and I kept trying to see into the parking lot, but it was impossible. The venetian blinds were halfway closed and the windows beyond were filthy.

Mike and I sipped our coffee.

I looked at my watch so many times during the next ten minutes that Mike said I was making him more nervous than he already was.

At long last, a bell tinkled as the door opened. I craned my neck up.

"Is it—" Mike started to ask.

I shook my head and sat down. "Just some guy." We watched a middle-aged man take a seat at the center of the counter and accept coffee from Verna. He ordered a doughnut, pulled out a newspaper, and began to read.

I sighed.

Immediately the bell tinkled again.

I jerked my head up. Then I grabbed Mike's hand. He stood partway up and looked over his shoulder.

The woman who stood hesitantly in the doorway and removed a huge pair of sunglasses did not look much like the Mommy I remembered. She was old. Her dull reddish hair, which was close-cropped but still managed to escape in all directions, was streaked with gray. Her lined face was a pasty sort of color, the freckles all running into each other, and her mouth looked pinched. It was a prune made of human flesh. She was very thin.

Mom's eyes flicked nervously to Verna and the men

at the counter. She seemed to size them up. When she was satisfied, she pulled the door closed behind her and stepped inside.

I couldn't stand it any longer.

"Mom?" I said.

She jerked her head around. "Maggie?"

"It's me, Mom."

"And me." Mike stepped out of the booth.

Our mother put her hand to her mouth and walked slowly toward us. "Oh, it can't be," she whispered. Her hand was shaking. "My babies. You're... Of course I knew you'd be grown up, but still, I didn't expect... Why, Maggie, you're beautiful."

She held her arms out to us and gathered Mike and me into an awkward three-person hug, murmuring our names and stroking our hair. When at last we disentangled ourselves, all three of us were crying, and so was Verna behind the counter. The four men had turned to watch, and even the young guy looked teary. When I glanced up, the four of them ducked their heads and spun their stools back to their food.

"Come on, sit down," I whispered to Mom.

She looked flustered and eased herself in on Mike's side of the booth, then rose and sat down next to me.

Verna filled her coffee cup wordlessly and returned to the counter.

Mom gripped my hand and twined her fingers between mine. "Oh, my God. How do I know where to begin?" she asked.

I giggled nervously. "I don't know where to begin either."

"Well," said Mike, "I'm going to college this fall. I got into Rutgers. I'm going to study math. And science. I might go into engineering."

Mom's hand returned to her mouth. "Oh, my God," she said again. "When I—the last time I saw you, you were...so *litt*le. I can't believe..."

I couldn't think of anything to tell my mother that was as exciting as Mike's news. At last I whispered, "I have a boyfriend. His name is David. Have I mentioned him in my letters? He's really nice."

"That's wonderful, sweetheart," said Mom, but she was frowning slightly. I wasn't sure what was wrong.

Verna approached us again, menus in hand. "You folks like anything to eat?" she asked.

We looked around at each other, shaking our heads.

"I guess not," said Mom. "Thanks."

Verna topped off our coffee cups, then left again.

"Mom, what about you?" I asked. "How's the pottery? Are you going to enter shows or something? I mean, what have you been *do*ing?"

Mom had raised her cup halfway to her lips, but returned it to the saucer untouched, then massaged her forehead, her eyes closed. "Kids, listen. I did ask you to meet me here because I wanted to see you after all these years."

Mike and I nodded.

"But," she continued, "there's more to it." She stopped speaking. Mike and I glanced at each other. "I don't know what your father has told you about the reasons for our divorce, but I suspect you haven't heard very good things....Am I right?"

I shrugged. Mike stared into his coffee.

"I thought as much." Mom's right eye began to twitch. "Well," she said, "to hell with him. I'll tell you something, babes. Your father's a dirty player. Do you hear me?" Her voice was rising slightly. I tried to pull my hand out of hers, but she gripped it tighter. "A dirty player," she repeated, more to herself than to us. "Yessir.... He always was, too. You ought to be aware of that if you're going to live with him. His little Leigh ought to know that, too. Forewarned is forearmed, as they say.

"Your father thinks that just because he earns a big salary he can throw his weight around, step on the little people."

"That is not true," I exclaimed.

"So you're on his side," said Mom quietly.

I tried again to wrestle my hand away. "I'm—I'm not taking sides," I replied, confused.

"Well, you always did love him more than me, anyway." Mom didn't just let go of my hand then, she practically threw it away.

I rubbed my wrist.

"So this is why you asked us here?" said Mike tightly. "To slander our father? You could have done that in one of your postcards."

"No, young man, that is not why I asked you here." Mom mimicked his tone of voice.

"Why, then?" I demanded.

"Because I have a present for you. Your crazy old mother is not as bad a person as you think. Believe it or not, I know what you've been going through the last few weeks and I cared enough to do something about it."

"The last few weeks?" I repeated in a whisper.

"Of course. You'd have to be blind, deaf, and dumb not to know that Courtenay Louise Ellis is missing."

"Oh, my God. Oh, my God," I said.

Mike dropped his head into his hands.

"What are you kids, crazy? I didn't *take* her," cried Mom.

"*Shhh,*" I hissed, looking over at the counter. Verna was scrubbing one of the grills vigorously. The boy had left. The two older men had their backs to us and were concentrating on a game of chess. The middle-aged man was wiping his mouth with a paper napkin. Then he slapped two dollar bills on the counter and strode out of the diner, his newspaper tucked under his arm.

"What are you talking about?" I said through clenched teeth.

"I found her, that's all. I conducted my own little search and I found her—a lot faster than all your cops and private detectives."

"Where is she?" said Mike at the same time I asked, "Why?"

Mom ignored Mike's question. "What do you mean, 'why'? What kind of gratitude is that?"

"If you're so mad at Dad, why would you go to all the trouble of searching for the child he had by another wife?"

"I didn't do it for *him*, I did it for you. I know how you two love that kid."

"How'd you find her?" Mike wanted to know.

Under the table, Mom's foot was tapping incessantly. Her right eye was twitching away a mile a minute. "What is this, the Inquisition?" She gave a little laugh. "I *found* her, that's all. I saw her on the street—with some woman."

Mike was getting to his feet. "Well, where is she?"

"Mike," I said, "I don't think Mom—"

"I don't care how she found her," said Mike. "If Courtie's here somewhere, we have to get her home. Now." He turned to our mother. "Where is she?"

The door to the diner opened and I glanced up. I realized Verna was looking at us.

"Keep your voices down," I said. "We're creating a scene."

Mom's foot stopped tapping. Mike lowered himself back into the booth.

I watched the person who was entering the diner. It was the man with the newspaper again. I wondered what he'd forgotten. But this time he didn't head for the counter. He strode briskly toward our booth. When he reached it, he withdrew a leather holder from his breast pocket and snapped it open in Mom's face.

She jumped back.

"Detective Harris," said the man. "State police. You're under arrest, Mrs. Ellis, charged with kidnapping."

I stopped listening and buried my head in my arms.

I sat that way while the detective read my mother her rights, and while he led her out of the diner. I sat that way until someone touched my shoulder and said, "Come on, Maggie. Let's go home."

Slowly I raised my head. It was Lamberton.

"She didn't do it," I said. My throat was dry and I took a swallow of cold coffee. "She didn't do it. She found Courtie for us. That's what she said."

"No," said Lamberton gently. "We've got Courtenay. We've had her ever since your mother walked into the diner. She told us everything."

I nodded numbly.

"Come on," said Lamberton again. "Mike's in your car. The police will worry about your mother. It's time to take your sister home."

18

Together Again

They took our mother away in a police car. The car pulled out of Annie's parking lot, eased onto the highway, and disappeared around a corner a few moments later.

The parking lot looked like a scene from a movie. Apparently, the police had staked us out. Cop cars were everywhere, as well as unmarked cars. Officers in uniform milled around, and FBI agents talked in low voices.

I stood in the bright sunlight, shielding my eyes from the glare, until Lamberton took me by the elbow. "Don't you want to see your sister?" he asked. "Why don't you ride home with me? I'll have Detective Becker drive Mike home in the Rabbit."

I allowed myself to be led to Lamberton's car. He opened one of the back doors and helped me inside. Becker was there, holding Courtenay in her lap.

"Okay, sweetie," she said to Courtie. She placed her on the seat, gave me a long look, then left through the other door.

When I saw Courtenay, I managed to forget my mother. Courtenay was a mess. She was dressed in the same clothes she'd been wearing the day she disappeared, her hair was tangled and unwashed, her dirty face was tear-stained, and she smelled awful.

I didn't care. I pulled her onto my own lap, hugging her fiercely, and rocked her back and forth, back and forth, while Lamberton started the car, signaled to Becker, and drove off.

We left Annie's far behind.

"Courtie," I said finally. "I am so sorry."

"Where were you, Maggie?" Courtie's arms were around my neck. She was gripping me as if it were impossible for her to let go.

"I was looking for you. We all were. We've been searching and searching."

Courtie began to sob. She buried her face in my neck.

"I love you," I said.

"I love you, too."

Courtie clung to me. I asked her a couple of questions, still unable to believe my mother had taken her, but she wouldn't answer, so we sat in silence.

Lamberton kept glancing at us in the rear-view mirror. Finally I asked him a question. "How did you know where to find us?"

Lamberton carefully passed a car in front of him on

the highway. Then he replied, "Let's wait until we're at your house. Your father and stepmother are expecting you. We'll discuss everything then."

I let my eyes drift to the window. Billboards and stoplights whizzed by at an alarming speed. Courtie had fallen asleep, her arms around my neck, her head resting on my shoulder. One grimy thumb hung limply from her mouth.

When we pulled into our driveway, I could see Dad and Leigh standing impatiently by the garage. They ran out to meet Lamberton's car. Leigh flung the back door open before Lamberton had turned off the motor, and grabbed Courtenay out of my arms.

"Careful," I said. "She just woke up."

Leigh nodded, tears streaming down her cheeks.

"Mommy?" asked Courtie disbelievingly.

"It's me, sweetheart," Leigh replied, choking on the words.

Courtie greeted her in the same way she had greeted me. A fierce hug, followed by a confused, accusing "Where *were* you?"

As I had done, Leigh replied, "We were looking for you, baby. We didn't know where you were. We've been looking for *days*."

Courtie held her arms out to my father, an old baby gesture meaning, "I want you to hold me now."

Dad folded her against his chest and rocked her.

"Where *were* you?" she asked.

"Looking." It was the first time I had ever seen my father cry.

Lamberton followed us into the house. A moment later, Becker and Mike arrived. Becker, Lamberton, Mike, and I sat around in the living room, waiting for questions to be asked and answered, but the first order of business was Courtenay. Dad and Leigh took her upstairs to bathe her and change her clothes. Then Leigh fixed her a sandwich, which she barely touched.

"Do you want to take a nap, honey?" Leigh asked her, looking with concern at her pinched white face.

Courtie shook her head. "I want to stay with you."

So Courtie, safely wrapped in Leigh's arms, joined the rest of us in the living room.

I asked the first question. "How did you know?" I said to Lamberton. "What tipped you off about Annie's?"

"You did," answered my father quietly from across the room.

"I did?"

"Sorry, Maggie. I did something I've taught you and Mike not to do. I listened in on the phone conversation you had with your mother."

"Dad!"

"I hadn't intended to, but I was waiting for three or four people to call me back this morning, so when the phone rang, I assumed it was for me. I picked it up upstairs and realized you had already answered it. I was about to hang up when I recognized Jessica's voice. Since we'd been trying so hard to track her down, I didn't want to let her get away. If she hadn't given you directions to meet her, I think I would have broken in on the conversation and asked her flatly if she had taken Courtenay. But she told you where she was. As soon as you hung up, I called Detective Lamberton and gave him Jessica's directions. I told him you and Mike were going to meet her."

I nodded numbly and looked guiltily at Mike.

Lamberton picked up the story. "Becker and I left immediately to try to follow you, just in case there was any trouble."

"We alerted the FBI, the state police, and the police up in Ridgewood," added Becker. "And another detective here called Annie's to find out if either a Jessica Ellis or a Jean Farmer was registered there. Jean Farmer was. The woman who answered the phone told him which room she was staying in, and the detective radioed the information to us in the car as we were leaving Princeton. We reached Annie's just after you did, and met the state policeman who later arrested your mother."

"The guy who'd been in the diner? Eating at the counter?" I asked.

Becker nodded. "He'd been watching your mother's room from the parking lot. Annie's was already staked out. The police were around back. When your mom left to meet you, Harris followed her inside, and Lamberton and I went to her motel room and found Courtenay. We signaled to Harris on a transistor he was wearing. He and two FBI agents joined us in asking Courtenay a few questions, she told us

that Jessica was the person who had taken her, and
Harris returned to the diner. That was when he arrested your mother."

"Had Jessica and Courtenay been at the motel all
along?" asked Dad.

"No," replied Lamberton. "Jessica talked to us
briefly in the parking lot. Apparently they'd been
staying in a hotel in New York City, some old place
near the bus terminal. They just arrived at Annie's
this morning."

"But I don't get it," I said. "Mom told us Courtenay
was a present. She said she'd found her for us. Obviously, she was lying. I guess she really did take
Courtenay if she confessed to it, but why did she return her to *Mike* and *me?* Didn't she think something
like this would happen? Why didn't she just du—just
leave her somewhere if she wanted to get rid of her?
And if she didn't want to keep her, why did she take
her in the first place? None of this makes any sense to
me."

"Well," said Lamberton thoughtfully, "let me answer your first question first. Forget about the reasons your mother took Courtenay, okay?"

I nodded.

"All right. So she has your sister but doesn't want
her anymore. I think she really did want to give you
and Mike a gift. She's felt terribly guilty about not
being granted even partial custody of you and about
not being able to be with you all these years. Remember the green car that followed you through

Hopewell? That was your mother. She just wanted to *see* you."

"She was in Hopewell that day? Not in New York?"

"Apparently," replied Lamberton. "She'd been keeping an eye on you for a while. I think she was using the hotel in New York as sort of a base."

"Where was Courtenay?" I asked. "I don't think she was in the car."

"Probably in New York. We're not sure. Jessica couldn't risk taking her out in public."

"Alone in New York?" cried Leigh. "Sweetheart," she said, brushing Courtenay's hair from her forehead, "did the lady who took you ever leave you alone?"

Courtenay nodded. "She said, 'I'll be back,' and she locked the door. I was scared."

"Well, of course you were. Did she leave you food when she was gone?"

"Sometimes. I ate Twinkies. And candy."

Leigh grimaced.

"Anyway," Lamberton went on, "your mother trusted that you and Mike wouldn't even suspect that she had Courtenay. She'd been following the news accounts of the disappearance, and there'd been no mention of her whatsoever. She thought she could not only get rid of Courtenay safely, but make herself look like a good, concerned, worthwhile mother to you and Mike at the same time. She just wanted to please you. She wanted your respect."

"Oh, brother," said Mike. "And now she thinks that

we brought the police along to have her arrested. We look like really terrific kids."

"It wasn't your fault," said Dad.

"*She* doesn't know that," Mike snapped.

"But why did she take her?" I asked again.

"To hurt your family," said Becker simply. "Not so much you and Mike, but your father, since he wouldn't grant her visitation rights. And she was jealous and angry that you—all of you—had what she hadn't been able to have when she was living with you—a real family. I suppose she saw Courtenay's very existence as an insult added to injury. Not only could your father have another marriage after she left, and a happy one at that, but he and Leigh were able to have a child, one that they treated well and didn't battle over. Jessica's ultimate failure was in not being able to care for her children. What better way to break up your home than to take Courtenay?"

"But she gave her back," said Mike.

"Yes," replied Becker. "And only Jessica knows the real reasons for doing that, but I suspect that, past the actual kidnapping, she hadn't really thought about what she was going to do. And there she was, stuck with a child who had needs and gave Jessica all sorts of responsibility she didn't want. She had to feed Courtenay, find bathrooms for her when they were traveling in the car.... Imagine being cooped up together in a little hotel room for nineteen days. She simply didn't know what to do with Courtenay. When she came up with the idea of returning her to her

family and looking like a heroine to her children at
the same time, it must have seemed like a dream
come true."

I glanced at Courtenay, who was resting in Leigh's
lap, looking much more relaxed. One hand was holding Dad's and the other was at her mouth as she continued to suck her thumb. But when she saw me
looking at her, she removed her thumb and smiled at
me.

I smiled back. "Hey, Courtie," I said lightly. "Tell
me something. How did the—the lady take you? I
put you on the school bus the day you disappeared,
and Birdie said you rode all the way to school."

Leigh adjusted her position and began to stroke
Courtenay's hair. "Can you tell us what happened?"
she asked.

"Yes." Courtenay nodded seriously, then paused,
remembering. "When I got off the bus, she was waiting by the walk. She said, 'Okay, Courtie, today you
come with me.' And she pushed me into her car."

"The battered green station wagon," added Becker.

"Where was the car?" Mike asked Courtenay.

"Behind the bus," she replied.

"Apparently," said Lamberton, "Jessica had been
watching your family for about a week before she
kidnapped Courtenay. She knew, from one of the letters Maggie had written to her when the trip to Saint
Bart's would take place. By the time you left"—Lamberton nodded at Dad and Leigh—"she must have
known your schedule pretty well, and knew how and
when Courtenay would get to school each morning."

"But Courtie," said Mike, "why did you go with her? You knew she wasn't one of your teachers. She was a stranger."

Courtie looked slightly sheepish. "I thought it was okay because she knew my name. She even knew 'Courtie' instead of my long name."

Leigh gave her a squeeze. "Maybe you and Maggie and I will have a talk about strangers tomorrow."

I threw Leigh a grateful look.

"I guess Courtie should be better prepared for..." Leigh began.

"The big, bad world?" I supplied.

"Yes."

"Tomorrow," I said, "Courtie and Mike and I will show you how to play the Lost Game."

"Now!" said Courtenay suddenly.

I was surprised she wanted to play.

"Nope. Time for a nap," Leigh told her.

"*One* question," begged Courtie.

I glanced at Leigh.

"Oh, all right," she said.

"Let's make it the big one," said Mike, coming to life. "This is for the championship, Courtie. Are you ready?"

She nodded.

"What's your phone number?" Mike and I asked at the same time.

"Five-one-nine-five-five-five-two-eight-three-six. That's my phone number, that's my phone number," Courtenay sang.

Mike jumped up. "Okay! What do we have for our

new champion?... A self-cleaning radar range complete with fly swatter and remote TV control? All right! Give the lady a hand!"

Everyone clapped, and Leigh, smiling, led an exhausted Courtenay upstairs to bed.

19

Afterward

Things in the Ellis household calmed down after a while, but they were never the same again. Leigh and I got along much better. After all, in a way, I had gotten Courtenay back for her. Mike and I hadn't intended to, but that was sort of the way things had worked out.

And I told Dad I wanted to talk to a counselor.

"That's probably a very good idea," he said. "I guess I should have told you and Mike more—about the divorce, about Jessica and her illness, everything. I thought if I kept it from you and just tried to give you a better life, things would be okay."

"Maybe they would have been, if we hadn't seen Mom. But now that I have...I don't understand how—I mean, she did something against the *law*. She got arrested. My own mother."

Dad couldn't think of anything to say. He just put his arm around me.

So we found a counselor, a friend of Mrs. Simon's, believe it or not, and I see her two times a week. I think the talking really helps. I'm learning how to forgive Mom. Maybe someday I'll understand her, too. Brad as well.

Mom has been committed to a psychiatric hospital indefinitely. Brad is on some kind of probation and has to put in a lot of hours of volunteer work in the community and go to what he calls a "shrink." Things are better for Jane and Andrew. We all plan to take psychology next year.

Guess who else sees a counselor? Courtenay. The Monday after we got her back, Leigh took her to the doctor for a checkup to make sure she wasn't malnourished or anything, and he strongly recommended that she have some professional help in getting over her trauma. So Leigh arranged for her to go to the play therapist at her school for a half hour every day. The therapist has a dollhouse and puppets and crayons and things. Through "games," she and Courtie talk about what happened, and sort out Courtie's fears and anxieties. Courtie doesn't know she's seeing a therapist. She just thinks she gets to go to a special teacher every day. She thinks it's some kind of privilege. I talked to the play therapist once. Maybe I'll become a child psychologist myself.

When a local toy store sponsored a child safety day, Dad and Leigh had Courtenay fingerprinted. The prints might help locate her if she ever disappears again. Then Dad insisted that Mike and I be fingerprinted as well. "You never know," he said.

Mike and I really did show Leigh how to play the Lost Game. She plays it with Courtie often. We've extended it into sort of an Emergency Game. Courtenay knows what to do in the event of just about everything from a skinned knee to a volcanic eruption. The most important thing we've taught her recently is that if a stranger ever takes her again, she's to yell, *"This is not my mommy (or daddy)!"* at the top of her lungs. She likes to practice that because it gives her the chance to shout inside the house.

"Do you think we're overdoing it?" Leigh asked me one day.

"I don't know," I replied, "but I'd sure feel safe having Courtie around in an earthquake."

Leigh grinned. "Maybe we should back off for a while."

The funny thing is that since the kidnapping, Leigh has been less protective of Courtenay. I was afraid she'd buy a leash so Courtie could never be more than thirty-six inches away from her. Instead, she realizes that kids today *have* to be prepared. She's still fussy about dirt and candy and bedtime, but she's pushing Courtie to be independent. And Courtie is the one rebelling at this. At first she refused to let Leigh or Dad or Mike or me out of her sight. One of us had to be with her at all times. School was a trial. And she wouldn't ride the bus after the kidnapping—not until Birdie began to bribe her: "If you get on the bus by yourself, you can beep the horn." Things like that. Courtie is getting better slowly.

Two things changed at Courtenay's school. One, now the teachers meet the buses at the curb and personally escort the kids all the way into their classrooms. Two, any absent child is checked on immediately. They've arranged a call-back system. If parents can't be reached, there's a list of other people to call to find out about the child. The teachers sincerely hope that nothing like the kidnapping will happen at their school again.

"But you can't prevent it," I said to Leigh one day. And she agreed with me.

Getting back into a routine was hard for me after Courtie was returned to us. I couldn't pay attention in school. I was lost in my courses anyway, because of missing so much homework, and I couldn't even take most of my final exams. But it didn't really matter. I was signed up for summer school.

The one good thing about the end of the school year was the Junior Prom. I went with David. Leigh and I had gone shopping, and she'd helped me find a dress pretty much like the one I'd daydreamed about. It was soft and white with spaghetti straps and a full skirt. Then we bought gold sandals, and a lacy shawl in case the evening was cool.

On the night of the prom, David came to the door bringing me a yellow corsage—and a gift. "For no special reason," he said.

We went into the den so we could have privacy. Inside the little box was a gold necklace with a heart-shaped locket hanging from it. I snapped apart the locket—and found tiny pictures of David and me.

"Because we belong together," said David.

He fastened the clasp behind my neck, and then we wrapped our arms around each other. Our lips met softly.

When we left the house that evening, everyone saw us off. I looked at them carefully: Dad, Leigh, Mike, and Courtenay, waving goodbye. My family. My whole family.